NEXUS OF SKYE

Beth Connor

WOLF GROVE MEDIA, LLC

Editor: Redd Herring, https://reddherring.com/

1st edition, 2025

Print ISBN: 978-1-958329-36-8

E-Book ISBN: 978-1-958329-35-1

PART I

The Raven's Descent

WOLF GROVE MEDIA, LLC

CHAPTER I

A vulture wheeled overhead, carving deliberate arcs across the washed-out morning sky. Birds were rare now, like hope. Lena had always felt a quiet kinship with them. They moved with the wind and she listened to it. Sometimes, when the grief crept close, she envied how easily they left. Somewhere deep in her bones, she remembered a world that was more. These days, the ground could split open without warning and swallow you whole.

She stood just beyond the boundary of the crumbling palisade, toeing the loose dirt and watching it rise in lazy puffs. The air was dry, threaded with the faintest trace of smoke - enough to make her nose wrinkle, and she turned her head, hoping. *Let her be safe.* Last time Mira left, she returned with a book that was covered in an unrecognizable script. Kashan had dismissed it, called it nonsense from the air, but the thing pulsed with a wrongness Lena couldn't explain.

A flicker of green light caught the edge of her vision, but when she blinked, it was gone. Storms with green lightning meant rifts, and rifts meant catastrophe. She tried to breathe through it, counting each inhale, but her thoughts circled back to Mira.

Mira, who never knew when to stop. Mira, who flirted with danger like it was a game.

For six long moons, Mira had bartered, traded, and foraged, pushing further each time. She did what no one else dared, all for the sake of the village. Lena had waited, watching the horizon every morning, telling herself not to worry. Mira was the strongest person she knew: sharp-eyed, iron-willed, and stubborn as a raven.

The vulture dipped low and cried out at a figure moving with quiet purpose across the brittle earth. Then the wind shifted again, carrying something Lena recognized instantly.

Mira.

She was already running, dust rising behind her in waves. The closer she got, the clearer it became.

"Mira!" Lena's voice cracked as she threw her arms around her. For the briefest, strangest second, it felt like a memory.

Mira's laugh was rough around the edges. "Miss me?"

"Every minute," Lena's face pressed into Mira's shoulder, inhaling the scent of salt and earth and ash.

Time bent inward and there was nothing else. Then the village stirred behind them, morning asserting itself.

Mira pulled back first. "How bad has it been? Any rifts?"

"We've held, but it's getting worse."

"Then I hope you've got room for some good news... And a bit of bad."

She adjusted her pack. "Good first: herbs for the healers, and seeds. Decent ones. We might actually get something to grow."

Lena's chest loosened. "That's better than we dared hope."

But Mira's face was already tightening. "Bad: The storms are different now. Bigger. People are heading south."

Lena frowned. "Azuros? That's - "

"I know." Mira's voice was flat. "The Slaver city."

Lena crossed her arms. "They think that's salvation?"

"They've run out of choices. I passed three groups. Some of them..." She hesitated. "They said they'd *been* here before. Like they're trapped in some kind of loop."

A shiver crawled up Lena's spine. "They think they'll escape it by going *there*?"

"They think anything's better than waiting to be swallowed whole."

She glanced west. "One of them mentioned airships patrolling the area looking for something."

Lena went still. "Close?"

Mira nodded. "We'll need to talk to Kashan. Make sure he listens this time. If the air-dwellers are moving this far north, we're not safe."

Then she pulled Lena into a gentle embrace. "But first, I want time with you. Tonight? Our spot?"

"The wind will be kind tonight." Lena replied, and for one suspended moment, the future could wait. Their reprieve ended when Elder Kashan appeared. His dark hair had started to silver, and his eyes missed nothing. He greeted Lena with a tilt of his head.

"Windreader," he said, before turning to Mira. "Wanderer. Welcome back. Was your journey fruitful?"

Mira straightened. "Yes, Elder. I foraged enough herbs to keep the healers busy for a while. I also found another settlement northeast of here. They're healthy, but their numbers are dwindling. Their elder isn't even nine-and-twenty. People are leaving the villages."

Kashan's expression darkened. "Maybe those who fled to the skies were right all along. Up there, they're safe." He paused, eyes narrowing. "Or maybe it's the land itself that's changing."

Lena tensed. "What do you mean?"

Kashan exhaled. "Sometimes, when the ground swallows a village, it's just gone, but there are stories. Structures that stand one day, vanish the next, then reappear, half-buried, somewhere else."

Mira scoffed. "Sounds like a ghost story."

Kashan didn't look convinced. "I think it's time to bargain with the Air Dwellers."

"No!" Mira's reply was immediate. "You'd sell us to the slavers? I'd sooner fight."

"At least we'd be alive," Kashan's tone was measured. "What do the winds tell you, Windreader? Will we survive another season?"

She could feel others pretending not to listen, but she knew they were. Windwitch was what they called her when she gave bad omens, and Windreader when they liked what she said.

Lena ignored it all. They just didn't understand. Most couldn't hear the wind the way she did. All they heard were gusts and howls. She heard voices. Layers of memory folded into the breeze. She hesitated, eyes half-closed as the air coiled around her ears. It spoke in layers. One voice was like cracking ice, another like a breath, and a third, faint and childlike.

"Time grows short. But yes, the winds still speak of healing."

Kashan let out a sigh. "Then we hold on a little longer," he said. "We'll speak more at the meeting and I will share my plan. Thank you, Windreader." He turned and walked away, leaving Lena and Mira in uneasy silence.

"Plan?" Mira asked.

Lena didn't have time to answer as a low rumble echoed in the distance. It was faint at first, then built steadily. She froze, eyes scanning the horizon. Then she saw it, just a glint at first: an airship cresting the ridge, its shadow stretching long across the ground.

Air dwellers, lords of the heavens, had little patience for the smog-choked surface, but they thrived above the poisoned clouds, where the air was still clean. The crumbling villages near the rift zones were easy prey. They never came without purpose. Some descended as traders, their ships heavy with luxuries or essentials. The cost? Tribute that left villages hollow and starving. Others skipped the pretense, taking what they pleased.

The slavers were the worst. They came cloaked in promises, dangling the dream of a life above the clouds. Those who believed them ended up in chains. The southern territories had already fallen, and Lena did not want her village to be next.

Mira's jaw tightened. "We need to get ready. No telling if they came to barter... or to burn."

When an airship came near, the village scattered, slipping into hidey-holes or vanishing into the hills. It was the only way to survive. The signal came, a low thrum from a horn carved of bone - not loud enough to split the air, just enough to slide under it.

Lena grabbed Mira's sleeve. "The old barn," she said.

At once, the village melted away, leaving behind nothing but sagging roofs and a cracked dirt square that dared anyone to call it a street. Lena and Mira squeezed into the dark space beneath the barn floorboards, pressed shoulder to shoulder. Every breath stirred the motes that hung in the stale air. In the dimness, Lena's hand brushed against Mira's cloak, then curled into the worn fabric, gripping it like an anchor.

They waited.

Overhead, the airship passed with a deep hum so close it made the floor vibrate beneath them. The sound pulsed, then faded, circling and searching. Stillness followed.

"They've matched me," Lena whispered. "Havenstown has a windreader now. Kashan thinks... he thinks if I have children, they'll inherit the gift."

Mira paled. "No! What about us?" The words tumbled out. "We need you. I need you. Why would Kashan - "

"He thinks we can build an airship," Lena cut in, "using Havenstown's old engine."

Mira stared at her. "An airship? We can't even keep the roofs patched. He wants to scavenge the sky with sticks and prayers?" Her whisper shook. "He's gambling with your life."

Lena flinched. "He thinks they'll leave us alone if we show we're not helpless."

Mira shook her head. "Helpless? He wants to paint a target on us. Air dwellers don't have allies, Lena. They have slaves."

The low drone of the engines swelled again as the ship circled back and the boards above them trembled. Lena swallowed. Mira's hand found hers, gripping tight. Neither dared breathe. The sound passed overhead once, then again, slower this time, and then... silence. They waited, motionless, until the tension drained from the air and the distant noise faded into nothing. Only then did Lena exhale.

"We're talking to Kashan after this," Mira said. "I'm not losing you."

"And if he won't listen?"

Mira's hand tightened around hers. "Then we make our own plans. Together."

Lena nodded, her gaze drifting toward the slatted barn wall as if she could see straight through it. "They didn't search long," she murmured. "It's almost like they weren't looking for a village at all."

A beat passed between them before Lena ducked out from beneath the barn, the daylight blinding her. She stood, brushing hay and grit from her clothes. Mira followed a moment later, somehow emerging with her usual calm, the dust never quite clinging to her. Overhead, the sky stretched wide and empty, but a thin line of smoke still hung low on the horizon.

In the square, Elder Kashan had appeared with his usual calm as he barked out orders. Around them, the village stirred as if nothing had happened: cleaning, sweeping, and mending. A child darted past, chasing a tattered ball, and a nearby woman muttered to herself as she sorted herbs in a basket. Lena and Mira exchanged a look. The world was shifting, but the village, as always, kept moving.

"It's like it never happened."

"It always is," Mira said, her eyes sweeping the sky one last time before letting herself relax. "If we just keep hiding, we'll die out. We have to do something before they find us."

"What else can they do?"

Mira nudged her with a tired smile. "Come on. Let's figure out what to say to convince Kashan that marrying you off is madness."

A passerby glanced at them, and Lena pressed her lips into a tight line. "Later," she said. "We'll talk about it later."

As they walked toward Mira's house, a small boy darted across the dirt path, all gangly arms and dusty cheeks. "Lena! Will you read my fortune?" he called.

Grateful for the distraction, Lena knelt. "Of course, little one. Let's find a quiet place and see what the winds have to say."

"You've grown, Derrick," Mira ruffled the boy's hair. "What are they feeding you these days - rocks?"

He puffed out his chest. "I help with the water wagons now! I'm strong!"

Mira's laugh was unexpected, drawing a few curious glances. An old man removed his hat and waved to her, revealing sun-weathered features. He called out to her, "Mira! Back already? What'd you bring this time?"

"Herbs. Seeds. Odds and ends." Mira shrugged. "Enough to keep us afloat a little longer."

Another chimed in. "You've got the best luck, girl."

"Luck's got nothing to do with it," Mira said, grinning. "It just takes persistence."

As the villagers drifted back to their work, Mira leaned close to Lena. "Funny, isn't it? A few smiles and a handful of words, and they forget how close we are to the edge."

Lena glanced at Derrick, tugging her sleeve, eager for his fortune. "It's not forgetting. It's hope and they need it."

She smiled and turned back to the boy. For a moment, the weight on her shoulders lifted. The winds would share what they could. Then the breeze shifted, and with it came a thread of pain. Lena's smile faltered, just for a heartbeat, before she smoothed it back into place.

"Come," she said, standing and holding out her hand. "Let's see what the winds have to share."

CHAPTER 2

Lena slipped out of bed, careful to avoid the creaky floorboards, and stepped into the night. Above her, the moon hung low, just a smudge behind the clouds. A rustle in the underbrush made her freeze. It was probably just a rodent, but her mind wasn't convinced. It conjured darker shapes: gleaming claws and teeth slicing through skin and bone. The noise grew louder and Lena tightened her grip on her dagger.

Then, with a squeak, a fat rat bolted from the bushes, darting past her boot and vanishing into the night. She sagged with relief, letting out a shaky breath. Lena hated taking a life, even when it could be food. This little guy would live tonight, but she knew it wouldn't last the week. Eventually, the hunters would trap it. Rats were easy prey and safer than chasing down the bigger predators that prowled.

As she continued down the road, Mira fell into step beside her.

"You're late," Mira teased.

"I'm careful," Lena shot back. "You should try it sometime."

Mira's grin widened. "Careful?" she echoed. "Lena, you wound me. I am the very picture of caution."

At that exact moment, Lena caught her boot on a stray root and stumbled straight into Mira's waiting arms.

"Sure... careful," Mira said, steadying her with a laugh, "about tripping over rocks in the dark, at least."

Lena scowled, her cheeks burning. "You're impossible."

"And yet you adore me."

Lena pulled herself upright. "Debatable." Try as she might to fight it, the corners of her mouth tugged upward against her will. They walked in silence; the ground grew uneven as the path narrowed. Lena's heart was full. Mira was here, and this was their time. Still, there was a strange undercurrent in the air.

"Do you feel that?" Lena asked.

Mira nodded. "Feels like the world is holding its breath."

Lena listened. The wind was absent, and the silence was too complete. A shiver crept down her spine, but as they neared their sanctuary, her tension lifted. Mira shook out a blanket, and Lena sank down on it. They lay back together, staring up at the endless, smog-thick sky, and Lena traced the faint outlines of clouds. For a breathless moment, the clouds parted, and a handful of stars burned defiantly.

The sight tugged at a memory she hadn't touched in years. *They're stars, Lena. Every one of them spinning through the heavens.* Her father's voice filled her head. Back then, the stars had felt close enough to touch. Now they were just pale ghosts of a world that used to be infinite.

"Something's wrong with the sky," Mira murmured, as if in a trance.

Lena turned to look at her.

"I saw a vulture earlier," Mira went on. "Flying in tight circles. Not hunting. Just... trapped. Like the air wouldn't let it leave."

"That's not normal," Lena replied.

"None of this is normal anymore," Mira sighed. "I thought the sun rose twice yesterday." She glanced up at the sky. "Time feels off, too." Lena had felt it too - the slow unraveling of the world. Then there was Mira: solid, steady, and still hers. She shook her head, willing the fear to loosen its grip, and turned to Mira.

"You're beautiful," she whispered, then leaned in and their lips brushed softly together. The kiss tasted of hope, but carried a pang of guilt, too. Before the desolation, love like theirs had been no one's business but their own. Now, every bond was measured against survival. Love wasn't forbidden, but it wasn't encouraged either. The future demanded strong children, not fleeting happiness.

"Where'd you go just now?" Mira asked, her brow furrowing as she studied Lena's face.

"Nowhere good," Lena admitted. "We should talk about my match. About what we're going to do."

"That's easy," Mira said, flashing a crooked grin. "Just say no."

Lena's lips twitched, but she didn't smile. "What if Kashan's right? What if more windreaders are the answer?"

"That's fear talking. Kashan doesn't get to decide what's right for you. Maybe instead of bending to him, you and I start our own village. We can't keep waiting for him to act, or waiting for superstition to tell us what to do."

Lena blinked, the words sliced deeper than she cared to admit. This was about her wind reading.

Mira caught the look on her face and softened a little. "Think about it," she said. "Our own place. Our rules. We'd build a real home. No airships, no bargains. Just... belonging."

Lena couldn't help the small smile tugging at her mouth. "And what would we do in this grand new village of ours?"

Mira grinned wider, rolling onto her side. "You'd be the elder, obviously. Wise and mysterious." She bumped Lena's shoulder. "I'd be the wanderer still, bringing back stories, trading supplies, eating feasts thrown in my honor. It would be perfect."

"You'd make a better leader than me," Lena said, laughing despite herself.

Mira rolled on top, pinning Lena, her hands braced on either side. "You're biased," she whispered, before leaning in so close her breath brushed Lena's ear. "You're my light. I love you."

"And you're the wind that keeps me afloat," Lena replied, her voice barely a breath. "I love you too."

For a moment, the world shrank down to just the two of them, then a piercing cry shattered the night. Mira froze above her, tension snapping back into her limbs. They scrambled to their feet, the air between them suddenly charged. The sound was unlike any predator she knew. Together, they climbed the slope, boots crunching dry grass underfoot.

When they crested the hill, a valley stretched below them, and there nestled among the rocks, was an airship. It was a hulking mass of metal and shadow, glinting in the weak moonlight.

Everything left in the wastes should have been stripped bare, gutted by scavengers or claimed by the storms. This ship looked untouched, as if it had landed minutes ago.

"What happened here?" she whispered.

She hadn't been this close to an airship in a long time, but the stories were burned into her mind - families torn apart and lives reduced to nothing more than barter. Lena knew those stories all too well, not from whispers around the fire, but from the hollow spaces her parents had left behind. The slavers had taken them when she was still small, and some part of her had never stopped hoping for them to come home.

Now, standing there, staring at the beast of metal below, she felt her legs lock. The airship was everything she couldn't fight and she reached blindly for Mira's hand.

"What do we do?"

Before Mira could answer, another keening wail came through the stillness.

"It's coming from the ship," Lena said, frowning.

Mira's hand drifted to her knife. The cry came again, fainter now.

"What *is* that?" Mira muttered. Her instincts screamed at her to leave, to turn and run, but she couldn't.

"Do you think someone is hurt?"

Mira shot her a look. "A lone person? Really?" Her tone was sharper than usual. "Air-dwellers don't travel alone. They have crews, and crews like that," she jerked her chin at the looming ship, "raid villages."

Lena frowned. "Maybe. But what if it's someone they left behind?"

Mira hesitated, the muscles in her jaw working. "You know the stories," she said, softer now. "That ship is nothing but trouble."

"I know." Lena swallowed hard. "But I couldn't live with myself if we didn't at least check."

Mira cursed under her breath, pacing a few steps, then swinging back toward Lena. "Fine," she muttered. "But if this ends badly, it's on you."

"Wouldn't have it any other way."

"Lead the way, bleeding heart." Mira shook her head, exasperated, and pulled her knife free from her belt.

The ship loomed larger as they approached, its hull crouched among the rocks like a fallen giant. Brass and copper machinery jutted from its flanks, gears catching the light. At the bow, a golden seagull perched, its wings frozen mid-flight.

A strange familiarity settled over Lena, like remembering a dream she hadn't lived. "How..." Lena breathed, boots crunching over brittle grass. "How did this even get here? We would have heard it land."

Mira's eyes swept the ship, sharp and wary. "Dropped out of the sky, I'd guess."

Lena gave her a sidelong glance. "Hilarious."

"I'm not joking. Perhaps they have some sort of stealth mode."

"They used to live by the ocean," Lena whispered. Her gaze drifted back to the figurehead, crafted with so much care it seemed it might take flight.

"Huh?"

"Seagulls. The bird at the front is a seabird."

Mira glanced at it. "It's pretty," she said.

Lena opened her mouth to respond, but a whimper cut through the air, close enough now to strip the last illusions away. They froze as the noise turned desperate.

"Is that - ?"

Mira cursed. "You've got to be kidding me."

They found her beneath the hull. A woman crumpled on the ground, her skin pale with sweat, and ice-blue eyes staring at the sky above and in her arms, a small bundle wrapped in a scrap of cloth.

"Shit," Mira muttered. "She's an air-dweller."

Lena dropped to her knees beside the woman and pressed her fingers to her neck feeling a fluttering pulse. The woman's lips moved.

"Please," she whispered. "Help... my daughter."

Her hand brushed the medallion at her throat, then fell limply to her side as her chest went still.

"No," Lena whispered, willing the life back into her, but there was nothing left.

She reached up and gently closed the woman's eyes then the baby wailed, a broken sound. Without thinking, Lena scooped the child into her arms. She was small and fragile, her tiny fists striking feebly against the cold. Lena rocked her, and the cries softened into hiccups against her shoulder.

"Lena," Mira said, her voice low and tight. "We can't take her. We barely have enough for ourselves."

"They'll come back," Lena said, steady. "That airship we saw wasn't looking for a village. It was looking for her."

Mira's face hardened. "Exactly. You think they'll just give up? If they come here, they'll tear the village apart to get her back."

Lena stared down at the tiny life cradled in her arms. The baby stirred, her small hand curling into the folds of Lena's cloak. "She won't survive out here," her voice cracked. "Even if the airship comes back, she'll be dead by then. She's too small."

Mira's hands curled into fists. "And if we take her? We won't survive either. You think Kashan's going to protect us? He'll see her as a liability. So will the others. You know how they talk. Anything that smells of the air-dwellers is a threat."

Lena shook her head, rocking the baby gently. "She's a child. If we leave her, she dies. If we take her… maybe there's a chance."

Mira paced a few steps, frustration radiating off her like heat. "A chance?" she hissed. "Hope won't feed her and it sure as hell won't stop the slavers when they come tearing down the walls." She stopped, turning back toward Lena, her voice ragged with anger and fear. "Do you want to bet all of us on a chance?"

Lena met her eyes. "I'd rather risk everything than walk away and let her die."

For a long moment, Mira said nothing. Just the sound of the wind stirring the broken grass around them, and the faint, hiccuping breaths of the child nestled against Lena's chest.

Finally, Mira exhaled. "You're impossible," she muttered.

"And you love me for it," Lena said, managing a ghost of a smile.

"Debatable," Mira grumbled, but she stepped closer.

"She's meant to be here," Lena said, meeting Mira's gaze. "She's a sign. The winds brought her to us."

Mira let out a laugh. "You want to tell Kashan that? That the wind whispered you a baby?"

"It's not a lie. Not if it's true in spirit."

Mira was silent for a long moment, her jaw working. Finally, she sighed, running a hand through her hair.

"We should check inside to make sure no one else needs help."

They crossed the groaning gangplank, careful with their steps. Inside, the air was stale, and the ship looked new and all the corridors were pristine. There were no bodies or signs of a struggle-nothing-ust clean, polished absence.

"It's like they vanished," Mira's voice was tight. The baby gave a soft, hiccupping breath. She didn't know what happened here, either.

After searching for the better part of an hour, they left the ship the same way they'd come. It felt colder now. Behind them the ship sat quiet and strange, like a thing pretending to be harmless. Mira glanced over at Lena, her mouth a grim line.

"We're really taking her?" she asked, but she already knew the answer.

Lena just nodded, rocking the baby when she stirred.

Mira let out a growl. "When this all blows up in our faces," she muttered, "I'm blaming you."

CHAPTER 3

The fact that Mira had stayed the night would trigger gossip if anyone knew, but it was not as reckless as what slept in the woven basket near the hearth.

"She's ours," Lena breathed to herself, dipping the soaked cloth again and holding it to the baby's lips. She latched hungrily, tiny fingers curling against Lena's wrist with surprising strength.

Mira, perched in the doorway with arms crossed and hair wild from sleep, snorted. "Oh sure. Two women, one baby. Nothing suspicious there."

Lena arched a brow. "We've been very productive."

"Oh, wildly." Mira deadpanned. "Is this the part where I claim I tripped and fell on an aroused blond-haired air-dweller?"

"You *do* have a type," Lena offered with a smile.

Mira exhaled through her nose and crouched beside the basket. The baby's pale skin gleamed in the firelight, and what little hair she had looked like it was spun from gold.

"She will not pass as mine, Lena."

Lena tilted her head, eyes still on the child. "People see what they expect to see."

"They expect to see dark hair and bronze skin," Mira said. "Not something that looks like the moonlight and starlight had a baby."

"Maybe she was born without pigment." Lena suggested. "It's rare, but not unheard of."

Mira gave her a look. "So, what, I was gone for six months, came back with a surprise baby tucked under my cloak, and no one's supposed to ask questions?"

"They will," Lena said. "But not many saw you when you got back. And you wore that ridiculous cloak. You could've been hiding half a pantry under there."

"I was hiding half a pantry under there."

"Exactly," Lena said. "People are tired, Mira. They're not looking to start trouble. And if they are, well - "

"I've scared worse," Mira shrugged. They watched the baby for a moment. Her breath came soft and even now, lashes like snowmelt fanned across her cheek.

"We'll say you gave birth too early," Lena said. "Elin helped deliver. We keep it quiet at first, tell everyone she's fragile, not ready for visitors. Let them get used to the idea of her before they see her."

"And... when they do?"

"We act like we're surprised by their surprise," Lena said. "Like they're the ones being odd."

Mira sat back on her heels, shaking her head. "This is madness."

"It's survival," Lena said. Then she met Mira's gaze, steady and unflinching. "And she's ours. That's the part that matters."

Mira reached out and brushed a fingertip against the baby's downy hair. "You're a terrible influence."

"I know," Lena said. "Now let's go convince Kashan."

They left just before dawn, slipping through the hush of sleeping streets. Only a stray dog watched them pass, its head lifting from a nest of rags before settling again. When they reached Kashan's door, Lena knocked with deliberate calm.

"Later," came his gruff voice, muffled by sleep.

"Kashan," Mira said. "It's important."

The door creaked open and Elin blinked at them, eyes falling to Mira's bundled form. Her brow furrowed, but she stepped back and gestured them inside without a word.

Kashan sat at the table, rubbing sleep from his eyes. "What's so urgent it couldn't wait until daylight?"

Lena opened her mouth, but Mira was already moving. She pulled the bundle from beneath her cloak and laid the baby on the table.

Elin gasped. "She's not - she's not one of ours..."

"No kidding."

Kashan stood, and his eyes narrowed. "Where did she come from?"

Lena and Mira told the story of what they had found the night before. A wrecked airship and a dying woman with a baby, no other survivors.

Kashan listened, arms folded and face unreadable. When they finished, he asked, "What were you doing out there? At that hour?"

Lena gave him a flat look. "Looking for herbs. Listening to the wind. You pick."

Kashan grunted. "Should've known better than to ask."

They let the silence stretch before Lena added, "We think the other airship from yesterday was searching for this one."

Kashan muttered under his breath. "A ship like that crashing should have rattled the teeth out of our skulls."

"Maybe a storm masked the sound," Mira offered.

"Or maybe it didn't crash at all," Kashan said. "Maybe it was placed there."

Lena didn't like the sound of that. "It doesn't matter. She's here now."

Kashan studied the baby like she was made from poison. "At best, she's another mouth to feed. At worst, she's a spark in dry grass. If the village sees her for what she is - "

"They'll whisper," Mira interrupted, "but maybe they'll believe she's mine."

Kashan barked a dry laugh. "With that skin? And that hair? Who's going to believe you had a baby with some ghost-pale air-dweller?"

"Not everyone's seen me since I got back," Mira leaned back and crossed her arms. "And I was wearing a big cloak."

Lena jumped in. "They might believe she was born without pigmentation. It happens." She didn't add how long it had taken for the village to stop side-eyeing her own pale complexion, and how the stares had only softened when her wind reading proved useful. "They adjusted to me, didn't they?"

Kashan looked between them, lips pressing into a thin line. "You think the village will just accept that?"

"They'll have to," Lena said. "She's here, and she needs us."

Elin had been silent, rocking the baby. Now she looked up, voice firm. "She is just a child. We will not condemn her to death for the sins of her parents."

Kashan exhaled. "Even if they believe you... there will still be doubt."

"Then anchor it with something stronger," Mira said. "A prophecy. Give them a reason to believe this isn't just a baby. Make them see a symbol."

Kashan turned to Lena. "Could you do it?"

Lena didn't answer at first. In the past, she'd twisted wind readings into things people needed to hear, but this was different. This was a lie dressed as destiny. "I could," she said. "But it's a dangerous line to cross."

"The wind will forgive you," Elin said, still cradling the child.

Lena wasn't sure. As she nodded, something shifted inside her. The breeze that was usually present at the edge of her senses was now silent.

"If the child is to be mine," Mira added, "I have a request."

"Ask it," Kashan replied, though his expression darkened.

"The airship must be part of the reading Lena gives. When the villagers accept her words, we'll find the wreck. I will be its captain, not you."

Kashan snorted. "And what do you know about piloting an airship?"

Mira's lips curled into a dangerous smile. "I don't need to know how to pilot it. I just need to own it."

There was something in Mira's voice Lena did not like.

Kashan's frown deepened into a scowl. "You're making a lot of assumptions. We don't even know if it's repairable, let alone capable of flight."

"We'll make it work."

This wasn't like her. Mira had always dismissed Kashan's airship schemes as reckless fantasies. Now, she spoke of a scheme of her own.

Kashan crossed his arms, studying Mira. "Agreed on one condition. Whatever you get when flying, you share it with the village. Food, materials, medicine. Everything."

Mira gave a dangerous smile. "Fine. But I have a another condition of my own."

"Of course you do."

"Lena comes with me," Mira stated. "You won't send her away to marry some stupid windreader."

Kashan's voice turned thunderous. "You - "

"Don't," Mira cut him off. "You're getting everything you've always wanted. An airship. The village prospers, but I don't leave without her."

The room went still as Kashan glared at Mira.

"Fine," he said. "But the truth doesn't leave this room. Do you hear me?"

He wasn't finished. "Once we start down this path, we never speak of it again. Not a word to anyone, no matter what happens. Hope is a dangerous thing."

Mira narrowed her eyes. "Understood."

Lena bit her lip to keep the question from escaping. Dangerous? How could hope ever be dangerous?

***

The days leading up to the council meeting passed in practiced coordination. Mira stayed out of sight, cloaked in her new role as mother, and Lena honed the story like a blade. If the council didn't believe her, everything would fall apart.

Just as they'd agreed, Elin and Kashan kept their distance. They didn't ask what Lena planned to say, and she didn't offer it. Plausible deniability was its own kind of armor. At first light, the council gathered in the longhouse. Kashan, Elin, and four elders settled around the worn table at the center as Lena stood before them.

"The winds have spoken," she said. "They have revealed an airship hidden in the wastes. It waits for us as a gift and a means of salvation." When the words left her, a breeze stirred at her back. The elders exchanged glances and Lena pressed on. "This ship could change our fate. It can carry us beyond the barren lands, bring us what we can no longer scavenge."

Kashan leaned back, arms crossing over his chest. "An airship," he intoned. "And the winds told you this?" His voice was skeptical, but Lena knew him well enough to hear the deliberate performance beneath it.

"They did," she said. "But that's not all." She let the pause settle just long enough to draw breath. "The winds have also delivered a child." That got their attention. The shift in the room was subtle, but it was there. "She is of us," Lena continued. "Mira bore her under the guidance of Elin, who served as midwife. The birth was premature, but the child lives." She felt the lie take root even as she spoke it. Not a sharp-edged thing, more like moss creeping in.

All eyes turned to Elin. She didn't flinch. "It's true. The child came quickly, but she is healthy."

Lena kept going. "The winds carried with her a message: The Raven's offspring will lead us to salvation. Her birth marks the planting of seeds long buried. From her, our future will take flight."

Elder Luc grunted. "This Raven - who is that meant to be?"

Lena lifted her chin. "Mira. Before my father passed, he always called her Little Raven."

Luc leaned back with a quiet hmm. "A curious name. And a more curious prophecy."

"It's a lot to ask," Kashan said at last. "An airship, a child, a prophecy. All in one breath."

"It's not for us to question the winds," Lena said. "But it is for us to choose whether we act. If we turn from this, we may not get another chance. If we do nothing, we fade."

Another silence stretched, then Elin spoke again. "You're certain this vision came from the winds?"

Lena met her gaze. "As certain as I am standing here." She hated how easily the lie slid from her lips.

The elders murmured among themselves. Debate rose in threads, too quiet to follow. Lena waited, hands clasped behind her back. At last, Kashan lifted a hand, and the room stilled. "This ship you've spoken of is only a story. We can't take it to the people without proof."

Lena nodded, already prepared. "Then send a search party with me. The winds have shown me where to look."

Kashan studied her for a long moment, then gave the smallest of nods. The breeze stirred again, cool against her cheek, but it said nothing.

***

A few days later, the villagers gathered in the meeting square. The search party had returned, their discovery undeniable. Word had spread like wildfire, and now every soul buzzed with questions. Lena stepped onto the rickety platform, willing her voice not to betray her. Mira stood a few paces behind, the baby in her arms.

"My people," Lena began. "The winds have guided us once again. There is an airship in the wastes waiting for us. It will change our lives."

The crowd shifted.

"And that is not all." Lena turned and Mira stepped forward and peeled back her cloak to reveal the bundled child in her arms. "The winds have blessed us with this child," Lena said. "Born of Mira, she carries a prophecy."

Kashan's voice cut through the hush. "And what words did the wind whisper to you?"

Lena kept her gaze steady. "The Raven's offspring will lead us to salvation. Her arrival marks the planting of seeds long buried. From her, the rift in our world will heal... or crack. We must nurture her." The words hung in the stillness. Not just hope, stakes. That was what they needed to understand. The cost of doing nothing.

"What's a raven?" someone called out.

"A raven is a bird," Lena said. "A creature of change and rebirth. Mira, who represents The Raven, has brought us this child as proof the winds have not turned away from us, but they won't carry us alone. We must act."

A sharper voice rang out. "And how exactly did Mira have a baby? She's barely been back a month!"

Mira didn't flinch. "Same way anyone has a baby," she said, raising a brow. "I laid with someone, carried her, and then gave birth. What, you need a chart?" That got a few uneasy chuckles, but it cracked the tension.

"She's small because she came early," Mira added, calmer now. "Elin was with me when she arrived. We didn't announce it right away because she was fragile, and because... well, you lot are as kind and welcoming as I remember."

A few heads turned. No one met her gaze.

Lena stepped in, gesturing to the child. "Her name is Skye. A symbol of the heavens and possibility. As we prepare for the airship, she reminds us of the future we could build. She is proof the winds still speak." Lena meant it. Maybe not the facts, but the feeling. She wasn't trying to control them. She was trying to give them something worth following. Something that wasn't just scraping by, year after year. If hope had to wear the shape of a lie, then let it be one that dared to stand.

A woman in the front frowned. "Why is her skin so pale?"

Another squinted. "And that hair... is that silver? Like in the old world?"

The old world again, like a myth they didn't believe but never quite forgot.

"It's the touch of the winds," Lena said. "A blessing. A sign she carries something new into this world. Something we've forgotten how to hope for."

Mira lifted the baby higher. "We need hands," she said. "We need hearts. The ship won't rise on faith alone."

For a beat, the crowd held still. Then someone stepped forward. Then another. One by one, hands lifted.

Lena stood tall. "Thank you. Now, let us prepare."

CHAPTER 4

The airship loomed above them, a shadow stretching long across the dust. Its frame stood undamaged, as if it hadn't crashed but simply arrived. Most of the work had gone into clearing the debris around it and carving out space for the crew they were assembling. In just a few days, the volunteers had turned the site into a humming hive. Ropes pulled taut with satisfying snaps, gears clicked into motion like the ship had just been waiting to be asked. No one said it, but this wasn't a repair. This was waking something up.

"It's almost too easy," one man eyed a pulley that responded like it had been freshly oiled.

"Things that come easy usually bite you later," a woman shot back as she wrestled a coil of rope into place.

Lena had heard versions of that same exchange a dozen times already. Most she tuned out, but then -

"I want to help!" A small voice cut through the din. At the base of the ramp stood Derrick with arms folded and hair sticking up at odd angles. He looked like a stubborn weed that had sprouted between stones. Too small to carry a pack, yet standing like he could lift the ship himself. "I can tie knots," he said. "And Kashan says I'm the fastest runner in the village."

Mira didn't even slow her pace. "You're also the smallest."

"Which means I can fit in places *you* can't," he countered.

After pausing halfway up the gangplank, Mira planted a hand on her hip. "We're not bringing you, Derrick. This isn't some adventure story."

"I don't care." His chin tilted higher. "I helped my parents, before they - " His voice caught, but then he squared his shoulders again. "Before they were gone."

Mira let out a long sigh and looked at Lena. "He's five."

"Six," Lena stood beside her. "But yeah. I get it."

Before either of them could come up with a firmer no, Skye's wail pierced the air. Derrick was already moving. He darted up the ramp like a flash of motion. Lena took a step forward. He was too small. What if he dropped her? He didn't. He knelt beside the basket, tiny hands steady as he reached for the baby. He didn't lift her, just touched her cheek with one hand and hummed, more feeling than melody. Skye's cries faltered. Hiccups. A sniffle. Then silence.

Mira blinked. "How...?"

"She was just lonely," Derrick said, not looking up. His hand moved over Skye's silver-soft hair.

Lena met Mira's gaze. No words passed, but the decision had already shifted. If they were going to have a baby on the ship, a playmate would be nice.

Mira blew out a breath and threw her hands in the air. "Fine. You can come. But you follow orders. No touching anything unless I say so. And if I catch you wandering off, I'll tie you to the mast myself. Clear?"

Derrick lit up, his entire face beaming. "Yes, ma'am!"

"Don't call me ma'am either." Mira waved him toward the others. "Go. Make yourself useful."

The crew didn't so much welcome Derrick as absorb him. Someone handed him a small coil of rope and a loose pat on the back; another tousled his hair, earning a quick scowl he tried to hide. He didn't smile much, but his focus was sharp and he moved with the stubborn purpose of someone twice his size.

Lena stood off to the side, with Skye tucked against her chest, and watched him navigate the tangle of legs and rigging like he'd been born to it. There was a rhythm to him. Quick steps, nods, the way he tested each knot twice before moving on. She felt it then. Not quite admiration, and not pity. It was just that she saw herself in him, the part that had kept moving when everything else had burned.

Mira appeared beside her, expression unreadable. "Well," her eyes tracked Derrick as he passed a wrench up the gangplank without being asked, "he's good with the baby. That's something."

"More than something."

Before either could say more, the wind picked up, a sudden gust that howled through the rigging, sending loose ropes snapping like whips. Lena felt it more than heard it, the chaotic voice of the winds, like a thousand whispers colliding at once. The sky had darkened further, a bruised hue spreading outward from the storm front. Thick clouds churned, their edges frayed and angry, rolling in with an unsettling speed.

"That's a rift storm," Lena said, her voice tight. Her eyes caught flashes of faint, unnatural light flickering in the depths of the clouds.

The storm surged again, pulling at her cloak, and for a fleeting moment, she thought she heard something more in their disjointed voices. Anger. Were the winds angry with her? Angry about the lie she had told in their name? She swallowed hard, but the guilt clung to her, making her wonder if this chaos was her fault.

Mira followed Lena's gaze, her mouth tightening into a line. "Can we lift off and get above it?"

Lena shook her head, forcing herself to focus. "The ship isn't ready. We'll have to ride it out on the ground."

Mira's voice rang out over the deck. "Secure everything! Get the supplies under cover and find shelter!"

The crew sprang into motion beneath Mira's commands. Lena pulled Skye tighter beneath her cloak and turned just in time to see Derrick knotting down a rope with quiet focus. His hands moved with a confidence that felt older than he was, and for a flicker of a moment, Lena smiled.

The prophecy might have been a fabrication, but this coming together felt real. As if something larger than any lie had taken root in its shadow. She saw a flash of green right before the wind hit, slamming into the hull like a wall. Everything froze. The ropes hung still. The rain suspended mid-air like flecks of glass. Then time snapped back, and the storm was on them in full.

Lena crouched over Skye, bracing as the ship groaned beneath her and lightning cracked overhead. It turned the clouds inside out and the first drops struck the deck with a hiss.

"Storm's here!" someone shouted.

"Secure the rigging! Cover the supplies! Below deck, all of you!"

Crew scattered. Tarps flew, ropes cinched tight. The deck pitched, and something large clattered loose and skidded past Lena's feet.

She turned. Derrick was still on deck, wrestling with a length of rope that looked twice his weight.

"Derrick, leave it!"

"I've got it!" His face was red, his grip slipping. He didn't have it. The rope snapped free with a violent whip, and Derrick stumbled toward the edge.

Then Mira was there, hauling him back by the collar. "Below deck! Now!" He froze, glanced once toward the rope, but the look on Mira's face left no room for argument. He bolted toward the hatch.

The rain thickened, steady and seething. It should've gouged into the wood like it always had, and left pockmarks, signs of wear, the erosion of time, but as Lena looked down, it gleamed. She reached out and laid her palm against the planks. They were wet, but solid.

Her brow furrowed. "That's odd."

"You and the baby should be inside too," Mira stated, pausing near the railing and following Lena's gaze. "What's odd?"

"The rain." Lena brushed   her   fingertips   across the planks. "It's not... doing anything to the wood."

Mira crouched down.

"Maybe it'll start later? Or it's magic."

Lena shook her head and glanced toward some rope. The strands had already frayed at the ends. What if Mira was right? What if some kind of magic protected this ship? Did the Air Dwellers have spells or enchantments that kept their great ships intact? If that was so, how could they pass themselves off as Air Dwellers? Could she somehow figure out the secret behind this magic? Was magic how they had thrived? There were too many questions.

"Lena!" Mira's voice cut through the storm. "Get inside!"

Lena startled, and she turned and slipped into the cabin. Skye squirmed in her arms.

Mira pushed her way in behind them, shoving the door shut with a firm thud. The latch clanked into place, muffling the storm's fury to a dull roar.

"Move." Mira nudged Lena aside. She gave the door a firm push and tug, ensuring the latch held, then stepped back with a nod.

Lena stepped into the cramped quarters and paused. The space had changed. Mira had wasted no time making it hers. Strips of fabric were pinned to the walls like banners, and a lantern burned low on the desk. Its glow brushed over a feather Lena had given her and a shard of polished glass.

This had once been the captain's cabin, Lena guessed. Its shape was purposeful. A half-moon table jutted from the wall, a chair bolted beside it. Empty shelves lined one side, their surfaces clean, untouched by dust. She wondered what had been there once. Air-dweller knowledge? Charts? Instructions for magic she couldn't name?

Skye whimpered, small fingers bunching in Lena's cloak. The lantern flickered once, then again, casting the walls in a strange, brief shimmer. The air felt charged and Lena froze.

Mira looked up, brow creased. "You all right?"

"Fine," Lena said, though her knees still trembled.

She swallowed hard, glanced toward the sealed door. "Think the crew's holding up?"

"They're doing what they can," Mira replied. "It's a mean storm, but we've seen worse."

She moved toward the small porthole. Outside, the horizon was a blur of acid rain and shadow.

"Rain's coming down harder," Mira said. "Might decide to peel the deck right off after all. Journey over before it begins."

Lena managed a thin laugh, but it caught in her throat. "It feels different this time."

Mira turned, eyes sharp in the lantern glow. "Different how?"

"Angrier. Like something's watching. If a rift opens, we won't be able to stop it."

"Maybe, but storms don't last forever." Mira tapped her fingers against the cabin wall, a hollow rhythm in the tense silence. "We'll make it. One way or another, we will take to the skies."

Lena placed Skye in the cradle, and Mira reached for her hand, their fingers brushing before twining together. The touch was grounding, a small anchor against the chaos. Outside, the storm howled, but here in the cabin, it was them against the world. Her gaze drifted across the cabin until it caught on a faint seam in the wall, tucked beneath a shelf. She slipped her hand free from Mira's and crossed the room.

"What is it?" Mira asked, already moving to her side.

"I'm not sure."

Lena brushed her fingers along the edge until they caught on a latch. She pressed it gently. A soft click, and the panel creaked open, revealing a slim, weathered logbook and a small pendant. It contained three interlocking spirals that caught the light, and its metal seemed worn smooth with time. Lena reached into her satchel and pulled out the pendant Skye's mother had died clutching. Holding the two side by side, her breath caught. They were identical, down to the curves and spacing.

She passed them both to Mira. "They're the same."

Mira turned them over in her hands, frowning. "Not just similar. They were made together."

Lena opened the logbook next. The pages were dense with precise handwriting. Her eyes skimmed columns of notes and intricate diagrams. There were maps of layered spaces, sharp-angled intersections, with some labeled in a strange script. One word stood out, scratched into the margins again and again, as if whoever wrote it had been desperate not to forget. *Convergence.*

Lena ran a fingertip along the word. "Mira... what do you think it means?"

Mira's jaw tensed. "Nothing good."

They bent together over the pages, peering at a sketch that looked like a doorway carved into nothing, notes scrawled around it in a language that twisted and blurred at the edges.

"Overlapping planes... movement between layers," Lena read aloud, slow and uncertain. "It's like our language, but off."

"Layers like other worlds?" Mira asked. "Or floating cities?"

"Maybe." Lena turned to another page. The diagram reminded her of a gate, or a tear. "If they had this kind of knowledge and they could move between worlds, why not leave?"

Mira was quiet for a long moment. "Maybe they couldn't. Or maybe the other places were worse."

Lena closed the logbook. "If this didn't save them... what chance do we have?" No answer came.

Mira held both pendants for a moment longer, then looked at Skye, asleep in Lena's arms. "She should have one."

Lena nodded.

Mira looped one pendant onto a length of cord and gently slipped it over the baby's head, and tucked the other one back in its hiding place.

"We don't have to understand it yet," Mira said. "But we keep it safe. Her most of all."

Her gaze lingered, though, and it was clear her thoughts were elsewhere. Mira's rough, calloused fingers brushed against Lena's cheek, the touch gentle. "You've got that look again." Her lips hovered just a breath away.

"What look?" Lena asked, her own hands sliding up Mira's arms.

"The one that says you're thinking too much."

"Maybe I am," Lena admitted, her forehead resting against Mira's.

"Well," Mira said, tilting her head, her lips brushing Lena's in a feather-light kiss. "You could stop. Just for a bit."

Lena pressed her mouth against Mira's, letting go of her tension, when a loud knock rattled the door. They both froze. For half a second, neither moved, caught between the moment and reality banging its way in. Mira muttered something that was not fit for Skye's ears and pulled away.

"One day," she grumbled, "we'll get five minutes."

Lena, half-laughing, tucked her hair behind her ears and stepped aside as Mira strode to the door. She yanked it open, cheeks still flushed, only to find Derrick standing there.

"M'lady!" he burst out, breathless and beaming. "The ship, it's unharmed! Not a scratch! It's like magic protected it!"

Mira raised an eyebrow.

"Yes! The storm tore everything else apart, but the ship doesn't even have a dent!"

"Good to know," Mira said. "Let's hope it stays that way."

Derrick lit up at the approval, then took off with a triumphant whoop echoing down the corridor. As the door clicked shut, Mira let out a quiet sigh.

Lena smirked. "You could've humored him a little more. You basically said the same thing."

"I *did* humor him," Mira turned. "That was me being kind."

Lena shook her head. "Still, he's not wrong. That storm should've left us in pieces."

Mira's gaze flicked toward where the pendant lay hidden, her brow knitting. "No," she breathed. "He's not wrong."

CHAPTER 5

The land had split during the storm. Not all of it, but enough. A jagged wound carved through the eastern edge of town where the gardens once stood, swallowing half a street and three homes without ceremony. What remained teetered close to the edge, the dirt crumbling in silent surrender. No one spoke of it. What was there to say?

As the time to leave drew near, the villagers gathered around the airship. Their faces held the look of people who had already lost too much and were preparing to gamble what remained.

Lena shifted Skye in her arms, brushing a strand of hair from the baby's face while Mira adjusted a winch line nearby.

"Think this'll work?" Mira asked.

"I don't know," Lena said. "But I hope so."

Nearby, Kashan tightened a bolt near the boiler, sleeves rolled and arms smeared with grease. He wasn't going, but he'd worked harder than anyone to get them ready. He stood now with a soft grunt, wiping his hands on a rag.

"Hope's not what makes a ship fly," he muttered. "Gears. Steam. Discipline."

Lena frowned. "Neither does giving up."

The crew returned from their farewells, each step heavy with what they were leaving behind. Some villagers watched from the edge of the clearing, a few waved. Others turned their backs.

Derrick hovered beside Lena, restless. "Are we just... leaving them?"

She didn't answer right away. "We have to," she said at last. But even to her, the words rang hollow.

Mira stepped to the helm, voice lifting above the wind. "All right! This will not be easy. We've got no maps or guarantees, but we've got each other."

The crew jumped to action, hands finding levers and pulleys like old instincts awakened. Steam hissed from vents, and the deck trembled beneath their boots. The ship responded. When someone faltered, a cable would groan in protest. When they got it right, everything clicked into place with uncanny ease.

Lena adjusted a line and felt the tension shift just as she moved, like the ship had guided her. "This thing's alive," she murmured.

"Good," Mira said, testing the rudder cable. "We'll need all the help we can get."

The sails snapped open with a sound like breath being drawn, and a deep groan rumbled through the hull. Below, someone started chanting. "The Owl and The Raven! The Owl and The Raven!" Lena stiffened. The words were meant as encouragement, but the lie she created stung.

Mira only smirked. "Let them believe what they need to."

"We're just two people," Lena said. "This isn't a story."

"Sure it is," Mira said. "We're just not the ones writing it anymore."

The ship rose. Slowly at first, then with a sudden lurch upward. Then the clouds thinned, a yellow haze parting to reveal a sky too blue. Far below, the town sat quietly, at the edge of a wound it might not survive. Lena held Skye close and watched. This might be the beginning or it might already be the end.

It hit her like a breath she hadn't realized she'd been holding. Lena stepped to the edge of the deck, stunned. This wasn't the sky she'd grown up under. This unbroken, impossible blue. A dream painted overhead.

Behind her, Mira's voice came quietly. "Lena... are we sure this is the same world?"

Sunlight poured across the deck, warm and strange. It touched her skin like a memory she didn't have. Around them, the crew stood, faces lifted, blinking into the brightness as if it might vanish if they looked away. It wasn't just a sky. It was *freedom*.

Mira clapped her hands, sharp and grounding. "All right! Stop gawking. Let's make sure we don't crash into anything."

"Crash into what?" Derrick squinted at the endless horizon.

The crew stirred back into motion, but Lena didn't move. She breathed it in the air like water after thirst. Each inhale made what they'd left below hurt more.

"What's next?" Mira asked as she stepped to Lena's side.

Lena hesitated. The crew was pretending not to listen. "We need to find an air-dweller ship. If we can convince them to help... maybe they know something. About this ship or fixing the land."

Mira raised an eyebrow. "Sure. We'll just walk up and say, 'Hi, we borrowed your relic, and now we'd like you to save the world.' What could go wrong?"

Lena gripped the rail. "You have a better idea? Wait for the ship to whisper instructions in our sleep?"

Mira leaned against a crate. "No. I just think handing ourselves over to strangers with skyships sounds like a good way to get tossed over the side."

Lena's eyes dropped to the cloud layer below. Somewhere under that white were fields that had turned to poison and homes collapsed into the hungry ground.

"If they had the knowledge to stop it," she said, "why didn't they?"

"We'll figure something out," Lena murmured.

***

Days blurred into weeks of nothing.

Below them the clouds changed shades but not shape. Gray to white to jaundiced yellow near the storm walls, but always the same in their quiet, crushing repetition. It felt like they were flying in circles through the same stretch of sky, caught in a loop where nothing waited ahead but more sky and more empty.

The food was going faster than she liked. Every time she passed the galley, she counted meals. Rationing would start soon. After that landing, which meant risk.

One morning, the clouds broke just long enough to see the ground below. The land below gleamed wrong. Fields drowned in chemical sheen. A building leaned sideways into the muck, its windows black with rot. Further off an airship, hovering low. Figures moved among scattered bodies like harvesters in a ruined field. They were not rescuers; they were scavengers. Lena stepped back, fast, before anyone else could see.

Then Mira spotted something in the other direction. Her voice rang out. "Look! Over there!"

"Another ship." Lena's voice was careful to match Mira's excitement, but she was nervous. "Our first encounter with an air dweller."

Its silhouette was angular against the endless clouds and it had none of the sleek elegance of their ship. Instead, it looked like it had grown in layers, each part bolted on with no concern for symmetry. The metal along its hull was mismatched, some panels smooth, others dented and worn like they had seen centuries of storms.

"How old is that ship?" Lena asked.

Mira squinted. "Hard to say. Looks like it's been rebuilt… but over too many years."

Moments later, a flashing lantern from the other ship broke the tension. It pulsed in a pattern, casting beams of light into the clouds. Mira squinted at the signal. "'Do you know what that might mean?'" She asked.

Lena shrugged. "Seems friendly enough, and it's better than starving." They would have to deal with the air dwellers sooner or later. It was their mission.

As the two vessels closed the distance, the air dweller ship extended a series of mechanical clamps. They reached out like metal hands, locking on with a clunk. Then, a grand sky bridge extended between them.

"We are supposed to walk over that?" Lena muttered, eyeing the bridge.

Mira smirked. "Well, don't look down."

"Didn't plan to."

Before they crossed, Lena turned to Derrick, who stood nearby holding Skye, the baby's tiny fist clinging to his tunic. "Keep her safe while we are gone."

Derrick looked at her like she'd just asked if the sky was blue. "Of course! Skye is always safe with me." He shifted his stance, as if to show that he was more than prepared for the responsibility. Lena bent down to press a kiss on Skye's forehead. The baby gurgled in her sleep, oblivious to the tension in the air.

They stepped onto the sky bridge, but for a second, Lena's foot didn't land where she expected, and then the wind screamed, tearing past her ears like a voice she couldn't quite understand. The message was clear - *turn back*. She jerked her head, expecting Mira to react. But Mira kept walking.

"Lena?" Mira's voice pulled her back.

"Nothing," she muttered, forcing herself to keep walking.

"Let's hope they're open to helping us," Mira said.

Lena didn't reply. Her gaze was fixed ahead, and she was focused on not plunging to her death. The other ship reminded her of a scavenger bird with a coat of stolen feathers.

As they stepped aboard, the scene was a blur of motion, color, and sound. Crew members in crisp uniforms moved with precision, while what could only be passengers in elegant attire drifted across the deck. There was an unspoken judgment that Lena could feel. The captain approached with a swagger that matched his robust build. His curling, dark mustache framed a wide grin, but his eyes were sharp as they swept over the newcomers.

"Welcome aboard the Skyward Seraph," he announced, spreading his arms as though to embrace the entire scene. "I am Captain Barnabas Hawthorn, at your service. It's not every day we host visitors."

"Thank you for your hospitality, Captain Hawthorn. I am Captain Mira Talbot of the... Raven, and this is Lena Davies, my windreader."

The murmurs rippled through the people nearby. Lena caught the way their expressions shifted.

"A windreader?" Hawthorn's brows rose. "Fascinating."

His gaze didn't linger on Lena for long. Instead, it flicked to the ship and the child in Derrick's arms. His expression didn't change, but something behind his eyes shifted.

"And the baby?" he asked casually.

Mira's jaw tightened. "She's mine."

"Ah," Hawthorn murmured, but the way he studied Skye felt like he already knew something they didn't. He gestured for them to follow. "Let me show you the heart of the Seraph. I trust it will be... instructive."

The Skyward Seraph was not what Lena had expected. Unlike their ship, it bore the scars of use. It had scuffs along its metal, faint discolorations, and scratches that marred its polished veneer. Inside, the corridors felt functional. As they moved,

Hawthorn's commentary continued. He pointed out the advanced navigation systems, the rows of armaments, and the massive engine room. Yet for all his enchanting words, there was a subtle undercurrent that left Lena's skin prickling.

"Not many women in command," he remarked. "Unusual, even among your people, isn't it?"

Mira's shoulders stiffened. "I am their captain. There is nothing unusual about it."

"Of course not," Hawthorn replied. "Though I imagine it must be... challenging, earning the respect of a crew."

"I manage," Mira said. Lena stayed close to her side, unease growing with every step.

"Here we are," Hawthorn said, stopping before a large, polished door. "My quarters."

He turned to Mira with an expectant look. "I would like to speak captain to captain," he said as he opened the door and cut in front of Lena. "Perhaps to hear more about how you've kept your ship running so smoothly in such... challenging conditions."

Mira's gaze didn't waver. "Of course," she said.

Lena pushed her way between them. "I'll stay."

Hawthorn raised a hand. "No need, my dear windreader. Our medical officer has been eager to meet someone with your particular gifts. Doctor Venn will give you a tour of the infirmary."

Lena didn't move. "I'm staying," she repeated, her voice firmer this time.

Mira placed a hand on Lena's arm. "Lena, I've got this. Go."

"Mira, I don't - "

"I'll be fine," Mira said, her tone leaving no room for argument. "Go with the doctor. Learn what you can. I won't be long."

Captain Hawthorn gestured toward the corridor. "Doctor Venn will show you to the infirmary," he said. "He's been quite eager to meet someone of your... talents."

A tall, wiry man in a pristine white coat stepped into view. Doctor Venn's polite smile was measured as he gave a small bow of acknowledgment before extending an arm to guide her. "Miss...?"

"Davies," Lena replied, not taking his arm. She lingered in the corridor just outside Hawthorn's quarters. Through the narrow crack, she could hear the low hum of Mira's voice.

Doctor Venn stood a step ahead and cleared his throat. "We should go, Miss Davies. The infirmary awaits, and I assure you, the captain will be well-occupied."

"I manage." Mira's voice carried.

Hawthorn's reply came dripping with condescension. "Of course you do. But imagine what you could achieve with the right support. A place up here, where you truly belong." His voice dipped lower, the rest of his words lost to Lena.

A knot of dread tightened in her stomach. Before she could think, her feet carried her back.

"All you'd need," Hawthorn continued, louder now, "is someone to vouch for you. Someone with... influence."

"And what would you want in return?" Mira asked.

"Only what you already are, Captain Talbot. Strong. Capable. Worthy of more than a dying world below."

His words wrapped around Mira like a noose, tightening, and her intake of breath sent a chill racing through Lena. She reached for the door, pushing it open without hesitation.

The scene inside hit her. Hawthorn stood too close to Mira, his body angled toward hers with a predator's ease. His hand was between her thighs and Lena's stomach churned. Mira's jaw was clenched, her eyes blazing as she held herself rigid, refusing to move or yield.

Hawthorn turned toward the door with infuriating calm. "Miss Davies," Hawthorn said, his tone as calm as ever. "Was there something you needed?"

Mira's eyes locked on Lena's, a silent storm raging behind them, and shook her head. *Leave,* she mouthed.

"Don't," Doctor Venn said, stepping into her path.

"I need to - " Lena started, but Venn shook his head.

"The captain is conducting an important discussion," he said, his voice dismissive. "It's not your place to interfere."

Lena tried to sidestep him, but Venn reached past her and pressed a button on the wall. The door clicked shut, cutting off the conversation - and her view of Mira.

"Miss Davies," Venn said, his hand still on the control panel, "the infirmary is this way. Shall we?"

Lena clenched her fists at her sides. Her mind raced, replaying Mira's whispered no. The door stood between them now, and she hated how powerless it made her feel. After a moment, she turned and followed Venn, her heart pounding in her ears.

The infirmary was a long, narrow room lined with gleaming white cabinets and counters, each surface pristine. Shelves were stocked with neatly labeled jars, vials, and instruments. A row of examination tables stood in the center, their smooth, paper-covered surfaces spotless and uninviting.

Doctor Venn gestured. "This is our medical bay. Fully equipped for diagnostics, treatment, and even minor surgeries. Efficient, isn't it?" His voice carried a note of pride.

"It's very... thorough," Lena said, her voice even, though her mind was still at the door behind her. Her chest tightened as Hawthorn's words echoed in her thoughts, and she couldn't stop picturing Mira standing there alone and cornered.

Venn opened a drawer and retrieved a sleek vial. He held it up to the light, his expression almost reverent. "Our nutrient serum."

Lena frowned. The liquid inside didn't settle the way normal liquid did.

"How do you make it?" she asked.

Venn smiled. "Trade secret."

Lena's stomach churned. Something about this place, about the too-clean sterility, felt... wrong.

"It is a balanced formula tailored to meet any physiological deficiency. Far more precise than the old methods." He continued.

Lena tilted her head, trying to appear engaged. "Old methods?"

He placed the vial back with care. "Oh, you know, natural remedies. Improvisation. Guesswork." He glanced at her, his tone mild. "Surely even you've moved beyond that."

Her jaw tightened, but she kept her expression calm. "We rely on what works," she said.

Venn nodded. "Pragmatic. Admirable, even. Though I can't imagine the success rate is particularly... reliable."

Lena forced a small shrug, unwilling to give him more. She tried to convince herself that Mira could handle Hawthorn, but the memory of his hand, the way he stood too close, was proving to be too much.

"This," Venn continued, pulling out a gleaming set of fine, needle-like instruments, "is part of our regenerative kit. Designed for rapid healing and cellular repair. It's fascinating what can be achieved when you remove uncertainty."

Lena glanced at the tools, but her mind was still elsewhere.

"Do you use anything similar?" Venn asked, his voice cutting through her distraction.

Lena blinked and looked at him, forcing her thoughts back to the room. "Not exactly," she said. "We make do with what we have. It's a matter of resourcefulness." Venn tilted his head, studying her as though she were an oddity. Lena bit the inside of her cheek, swallowing the retort that rose to her lips.

Venn turned away, continuing his tour with the same detached precision. "Efficiency separates progress from stagnation," he remarked, as if the observation were self-evident.

Lena did not hear Doctor Venn's voice anymore. It washed over her, devoid of warmth. She focused on the polished floor, where the brightness reflected her own uneasy expression back at her. Everything here felt artificial, suffocating. She couldn't stop replaying the moment Mira had told her to leave. Finally, he stopped beside a counter and pulled out a small case, presenting it to her. "A basic first aid kit," he said, his voice pinched with forced generosity. "Consider it a gift. Your ship might find it… enlightening."

Lena took the kit without comment. She wanted to drop it or throw it back at him. Instead, she just nodded.

The sound of a chime interrupted the tension. A light on the infirmary wall flickered from red to green. Venn glanced at it and nodded to himself, as though it had confirmed some quiet, internal decision.

"I believe the captain has concluded his business," he said, brushing his hands together as though the conversation had been little more than a chore. "Shall we go meet them on the deck?"

"Yes," Lena said, her voice clipped. She tucked the kit under her arm and turned for the door, moving quickly enough that she was several steps ahead of Venn before he caught up.

The walk back to the deck felt longer than it should have, the corridors stretching before them, and the moment they stepped outside, the light felt too bright. The plank between the ships was already laid out, stretching across the gap between vessels. A few of the Seraph's deckhands were crossing it, carrying crates of supplies to their ship with efficient strides. Then Lena saw Mira.

She was standing on the deck, posture rigid. Her hands were clasped in front of her, the knuckles white against her sun-browned skin. Her eyes were red-rimmed, as though she'd been crying.

"I do hope we can trade again in the future," Captain Hawthorn said, his voice oozing with smug satisfaction.

His smile was as polished as the rest of the Seraph, all surface and no substance, as he turned to Mira.

Mira didn't reply. Lena looked at her, searching for answers in her expression, but Mira refused to meet her eyes. She stared past Lena, her gaze fixed somewhere in the middle distance.

"It's been a pleasure," Hawthorn added, his tone almost sing-song.

Mira turned without a word, crossing the plank. Her stride was different, as if she had already decided something Lena wasn't privy to. When they reached their side, Mira hesitated at the threshold. Her fingers brushed the metal hull, her gaze lingering on the ship she had just left. Her jaw was set. Then, without a word, she stepped into her cabin and shut the door behind her. Lena exhaled, realizing only then that she'd been holding her breath. Mira hadn't met her eyes once. She started toward the door, but before she could reach it, it swung open.

Derrick stepped out, his expression heartbroken as he looked up at Lena. "She told me to leave," he muttered, then he shouldered past her and stalked down the corridor.

Lena lifted her hand, uncertainty creeping in. She should give Mira time. Let her breath, but then she remembered the look on her face, and she knocked. "Mira?" There was no answer.

Lena's hand lingered on the latch before she pushed it open. The hinges let out a soft groan as the cabin came into view. Mira was sitting on the bed, one hand gripping the side of Skye's cradle. The baby was asleep, her tiny body rising and falling with a rhythm that felt out of place in the tense air. Mira's other foot moved mechanically, rocking the cradle in slow, deliberate motions.

"Mira," Lena said, stepping inside and shutting the door behind her. "What happened?" Mira's head snapped up, her eyes locking on Lena's with a flash of anger and something more raw. For a moment, Lena faltered under that gaze, realizing what Mira had endured. The words shifted in her throat. "Why?" she asked. "Why did you do that? We didn't need supplies that badly."

Mira let out a bitter laugh. "Didn't we?" she said, her voice brittle. Her foot stilled, and her hand gripped the cradle's edge as though it were the only thing keeping her grounded. "We have nothing, Lena. No technology, no knowledge worth trading. What was I supposed to offer? Empty promises?"

"We could've figured something out," Lena said, desperation slipping into her tone. "We always do."

Mira shook her head, her breath coming quicker now. "Not with them. Do you know what Hawthorn said to me? What he saw when he looked at us? Nothing." Her voice was raw, but her eyes were colder than before. "And you know what? He was right."

"Mira - "

"No," she snapped. "We are nothing to them. I will never let us be nothing again." Her voice broke on the last word, and Lena's chest tightened. She moved closer, sitting down beside Mira and sliding an arm around her shoulders. Mira shuddered and pulled away. "Don't touch me."

Lena froze, her hand hovering in the space where Mira had been. "Mira..."

"What do you want me to say?" Mira's hands pressed hard against her knees, as if trying to keep herself from shaking. "That I'm fine? That it was worth it? Because it wasn't. It wasn't fine, but we had nothing else. Nothing!"

Lena's throat tightened. "There were other options."

Mira turned on her, her eyes blazing with fury. "There was no good choice. Do you think they'd keep us alive out of kindness? Out of respect? No. They're stronger, smarter, better equipped. And they know it. They only keep us around because we're useful. I made sure we were useful." Lena opened her mouth to argue but stopped, the words dying on her tongue. Mira turned away again, her hand falling back to the cradle, trembling as it rested on the edge. She brushed a finger over Skye's forehead. "It wasn't for the supplies. It was for her."

Lena didn't know what to say. The silence grew between them, broken only by the soft creak of the cradle as Mira started rocking it again.

CHAPTER 6

T he ship cut through the clouds, day after day, wrapped in the same endless gray. Or maybe not the same. Perhaps the clouds changed and only Lena stayed the same. She stopped keeping track. There were no hours. Just hunger and drift.

At first, Mira stayed in her cabin. Her door stayed shut through storms and meal calls, the space around it growing quieter each day. When she finally reappeared, she wore her smile like a shield, but it couldn't hide the hollowness behind her eyes. She moved through the ship like a ghost. When her patience cracked, the crew didn't challenge her, they just swallowed it. She had saved them, after all. Gratitude couldn't feed them. Supplies thinned again and the crew settled into a morose routine. Mealtimes came and went with barely a word. Still no sign of other ships.

Mira grew shorter with everyone. The crew started flinching every time she passed. Respect, Lena realized, had twisted into wariness. Even when it was just the three of them: Mira, Lena, and Skye, the change held. Mira touched Lena less and when she did, it felt rehearsed.

But she touched the ship. Lena started noticing Mira brushing her fingers along the railing, pausing mid-step to press her palm against the hull. She'd stand at the bow for hours, whispering things no one else heard, staring straight ahead like the figurehead might blink. It was the only time her shoulders dropped. The only time she looked... calm. Lena said nothing, but the ship seemed to listen.

Mira named Derrick as Skye's official guard, though Lena had a feeling it wasn't so much about trusting him as it was about keeping him busy. The boy threw himself into his role with pride. Lena often caught him fussing with Skye's blanket, smoothing it out again and again, or humming a lullaby while she slept. He tried so hard to act grown-up, but he was still just a kid and Lena carved out time for him to be one. She gave him a chance to explore the ship's corners, to play, to do whatever it was boys did when they weren't carrying responsibilities far too big for them.

Derrick was off somewhere below deck, prying up floorboards or poking at brass fittings like the ship was a puzzle meant just for him. Lena didn't stop him. He needed the space. Skye, warm and quiet in her arms, didn't seem to mind either. For once, the air held still.

She made her way to Mira's cabin.

Inside, Mira paced like something caged, her boots scuffing the floor with each tight turn. One hand brushed the hilt of her knife every time she passed the desk. The tremor started small, just her fingers twitching, but it climbed fast, until her whole body vibrated with fury. When she spoke, her voice cracked. "I won't beg them. I'll destroy them before I ever do."

Lena didn't say anything at first. She watched the storm move through Mira's body and waited for a pause. "Mira, not all of them are like Captain Hawthorn. You know that. We can't damn an entire people for one man's cruelty." Mira's jaw flexed, teeth grinding. A knock broke the tension.

The door creaked open, and Derrick stepped in, both hands balancing a tray of food. His eyes flicked from Lena to Mira and back again. "Here's your meal," he said, voice pitched too high. He set the tray down with a clatter.

Mira turned on him. "I am The Raven!" she said. The words snapped like a thrown blade. "You will address me as such."

Derrick froze, the light draining from his face. "Yes - yes, Raven," he stammered, tripping over his own feet and scrambling back toward the door.

Mira didn't move. She stood taller now, shoulders squared, the title settling across her like a second skin.. Something had clicked into place. She wasn't trying it on. She *was* it.

Derrick fled, the door left ajar behind him. His footsteps echoed down the hall, a ragged rhythm of retreat.For a breath, Mira faltered. Then she set her jaw and turned away, her silhouette already slipping back into the command the title demanded. Lena watched her. The girl she had once known was still there, somewhere.

Lena stared after him. "Was that necessary?" Mira's shoulders sagged, and the fire in her eyes dimmed as tears spilled. She sank to the floor with a soft thud. Lena was at her side in an instant, sliding down to wrap her arms around her. Mira didn't resist, though her body remained stiff. "Mira," Lena whispered. "I know you're angry. You have every right to be. But we can't let one man's actions unravel everything we've worked for."

Mira sniffed, swiping at her tear-streaked face. "I know. It's just... I didn't think it would feel like this. Everything we're trying to do - it feels useless."

"We could always land," Lena suggested. "Just to resupply. Maybe even barter. There are still ground dweller settlements - "

"No." Mira cut her off. "If we land, they starve. Is that the salvation you want?"

Mira turned toward her, eyes dark and unreadable. "We can't show up with nothing and beg like scavengers. Not to them, not to anyone."

"So what do we do?"

"We find another ship," Mira said. "And this time, we don't beg. We make them see us for what we are. Not desperate, not weak. If they don't give us what we need, we take it." Lena opened her mouth to argue, but faltered. The fire in Mira's eyes was back. Instead, she stood and placed a hand on Mira's arm, a silent plea for restraint. Mira didn't shake her off, but her expression didn't soften either. "We'll do what needs to be done," she said, her voice dangerously quiet. "For them. For us."

Lena tightened her hold on Skye and hesitated, the words forming before she realized she'd decided to say them aloud. "You know we don't have to follow it, right?" Lena whispered. "The prophecy. We could change it. Rewrite it. Just... someday."

Mira's hand twitched where it rested on the crate. "Maybe," she said quietly. "But not today."

"We knew this would be hard. But we can't let it change who we are. We can't lose sight of what we're fighting for."

Mira's eyes caught the light with a frightening clarity. "There has to be something on this ship we can use. Something to even the odds."

Lena hesitated. "It doesn't seem like the kind of ship built for combat. It's... different."

"Different," Mira repeated. "And yet it survived storms that should've ripped it apart. It's more than different, it's stronger. We just haven't figured out how yet." Mira glanced at Skye. The baby nestled against Lena's chest. "Fetch Derrick. He can watch her while we search."

Lena nodded and stepped into the corridor. It didn't take long to find Derrick near the galley, bent over a makeshift game he'd scratched on the floor. His dark curls bounced as he glanced up, his face brightening when he saw her.

"Can you watch Skye for a bit?" Lena asked. "Mira and I need to check something."

Derrick lit up. "Uh-huh!" he exclaimed, his excitement spilling over before he tried to compose himself. He took the baby in his arms. "She's safe with me." Lena smiled, brushing a hand over Skye's cheek before heading back.

Mira was already at the hatch. She didn't say a word, just opened it and started down the ladder into the lower decks. They had searched the Gull many times before, but the ship was never quite the same. It shifted, offering extra spaces that hadn't been there before. Hidden rooms, strange compartments (unfortunately never food). At the end of a hallway, they reached a storage room lined with crates. The air was cooler here and

Lena hesitated at the doorway. Mira wasted no time. She dived in with a single-minded focus.

"Here." Mira held up something in her hands.

It was a sword, though calling it that felt wrong. The blade shimmered, catching light from nowhere. Mira smiled like it was the most beautiful thing she'd ever seen. She turned the weapon in her hands as though it had been made for her.

"What is that?" Lena asked.

"Something useful," Mira replied.

They kept searching. Lena's hands found a cylindrical device with a smooth surface. She twisted a gear near its base, and it responded with a soft whir. "It's not a weapon," Lena said, tilting it toward the light and looking through the glass. "It feels like... a fancy telescope?"

Mira glanced over. "Great. Does it fire anything?"

Lena frowned, turning the device in her hands. "I don't think so, but it could help us navigate. Find new routes, maybe even see farther than we've ever managed." Mira snorted, already digging into the next crate. Lena shifted her weight. "Mira, what are we even doing here?"

"Surviving," Mira said flatly. The ship always seemed to offer what they needed, but it never felt like a gift. More like a test. Or a reward. When Mira ran her hands along the crates, the ship hummed beneath her touch, like it was waiting for her to find what it had hidden. And then she did. Lena stepped closer, hesitating before brushing her hand against Mira's arm.

Mira paused, and Lena leaned in, pressing a soft kiss to her forehead. "You are my light, Mira. I love you." Mira didn't reply. She turned back to the crate, her silence louder than any words.

***

The Raven seemed to feed on Mira's anger. Why couldn't it respond to compassion? Why couldn't it understand what Lena was trying to give it? More than once, she had caught Mira standing at the figurehead, her posture rigid, talking as though she were addressing the ship. And what unnerved Lena most was how the ship seemed to listen.

Lena had tried everything to achieve the same level of communication with the ship. She'd stood at the bow, her hands pressed flat against the smooth wood, whispering her pleas to it. "Please," she had begged. "We need food. Supplies. Peace. Not more weapons." The ship, as always, gave no sign it was listening.

It wanted Mira.

Now, with the clouds stretching around them, Lena closed her eyes, her fingers curling against the bow. "Please," she whispered again. "Help us." A jolt rippled through the ship. Lena stumbled as The Raven veered to the east. Her breath caught as she opened her eyes and saw it: another ship. Faint at first, then clearer as it emerged from the clouds. "Thank you," she whispered. "Let it be a peaceful encounter."

But the ship had already made its choice. Before Lena could react, a deep groan rumbled and panels slid open, revealing cannons she hadn't even known were there. She hadn't asked for this, but Mira had.

"No, no, no," Lena whispered. "We don't need to do this!" But the Gull wasn't listening. The cannons clicked into place as the other ship drifted closer.

Mira joined Lena at the prow. The charcoal smudged around her eyes gave her an almost feral look, and the sword at her side glinted in the light. The opposing ship had a hull that was painted silver, with sails trimmed in geometric patterns. As the vessels aligned, a tall man emerged onto the deck. His eyes scanned The Raven, lingering on the weaponry before settling on Mira.

"I am Captain Eldridge," he said. "What brings you to my ship?"

Mira stepped forward, her hand resting on her sword's hilt. "We need supplies."

"Thank you for speaking with us," Lena blurted. "We're trying to understand more about air-dweller society. You said 'my ship.' Does that mean you're not aligned with anyone else?"

Eldridge's gaze shifted to Lena. "Each ship is sovereign. We answer to no one but ourselves. Alliances are rare, and trust even rarer. Out here, every ship has its own laws."

"No governing body?" Lena pressed. "No way to build cooperation?"

Eldridge's smile didn't reach his eyes. "Cooperation is a liability. It's a weakness. Trusting another to act in your best interest is a fool's gamble. They'll always choose their own survival first." His eyes narrowed at Mira. "You already know this, don't you, Captain?"

Lena forced herself to stand firm. "Surely some captains see the value of alliances."

Eldridge chuckled. "Some might. Relics of a gentler age, clinging to ideals that have no place here. If you're looking for allies, good luck finding someone naïve enough to trust you."

Mira's fingers tightened on her sword. "We're not asking for favors. Just enough to get by. Food. Supplies."

Eldridge inspected the Gull's weaponry. "And what exactly do you offer?"

Before Mira could respond, a low hum filled the air. Lena froze as one of the cannons swiveled toward Eldridge's ship.

"Impressive," he said, his voice tight. "A fully operational cannon. Do you even know what you're wielding? This is not technology built for posturing."

Mira's lips curved into a predatory smile. "We take care of what's ours."

"Enough," Eldridge said. "If I give you what you need, will you leave us at peace?"

Mira inclined her head. "You'll never see us again."

Eldridge flipped a hand, and his crew moved swiftly, lowering crates onto the Gull. The supplies were modest, dried goods, barrels of water, and a few tools, but enough to stave off desperation. As the last crate was secured, Eldridge approached the rail. "You may have won this exchange, Captain Mira, but don't mistake power for permanence. Ships like yours draw enemies quickly."

"Then they'd better think carefully before crossing us." Without another word, Eldridge turned and disappeared below deck, and the ships drifted apart.

Lena stood frozen as The Raven thrummed beneath her feet. Her eyes lingered on Eldridge's ship as it receded into the clouds.

She wanted peace, knowledge, understanding, but it was power that had secured their survival today. She stood beside Mira at the rail, her heart heavy. "Well, we got what we needed."

Mira didn't respond, her darkened eyes fixed on the horizon. There was a hunger in her gaze.

When Lena approached Mira's cabin later that night, the door was unlatched. Inside, Mira sat on the bed, her figure outlined by the faint glow of moonlight spilling through the small porthole. She was staring out at the swirling clouds below. Lena hesitated before stepping closer, and she cleared her throat. "I know it's hard. But we can't give up. We'll find the allies we need without violence."

Mira's gaze didn't shift from the window. When she spoke, her words were full of bitterness. "Allies," she said, spitting the word as though it left a foul taste in her mouth. "According to the last captain, they don't exist. I'm tired of begging for scraps. If they won't help us willingly, we'll make them help."

The words struck Lena like a blow. "What are you saying?" she asked, though the answer was already taking shape in her mind, and it terrified her.

Mira turned to face her, her eyes dark and rimmed with the charcoal she wore like war paint. "We have The Raven," Mira said. "It's time the air dwellers saw us as a force to be reckoned with. If they won't listen, we'll make them."

"That's not who we are," Lena took a step closer, desperate to break through the walls Mira was building around herself. "We can't become what we're trying to fight. If we do that, we'll lose everything that makes this worth doing."

Mira's lips pressed into a thin line. The clouds churned below, as if reflecting the storm inside her. "Then maybe you don't see what's at stake here."

Lena's heart ached at the distance that had grown between them. "We're trying to heal the world, not break it further. We have to hold on to that, no matter how hard it gets."

When Mira spoke, her voice was icy. "Sometimes you have to break something to fix it."

CHAPTER 7

The ship had been too quiet all morning. Not peaceful, though, *unnatural*. The air felt stretched, and the sails moved without wind, shifting as though drawn forward by something unseen. Lena stared at them too long and felt dizzy. Then came the footsteps. Each hit like a hammer on glass as Mira strode across the deck.

"Get ready," Mira's face was locked into that expression again, too hard. The calm that preceded breaking things.

"For what?" Lena asked, but her gut already knew.

Mira didn't answer. Her eyes were fixed on the horizon and Lena followed her gaze. Out of the mist, another ship took shape. This one was all sharp angles, and no grace. "Skye's with Derrick. My cabin. Join them." Mira spoke without looking at her. It was not a request, but a command. Stay out of the way.

"You don't get to order me off the deck like I'm crew."

Mira's mouth twitched. "You're not crew. You're my second mistake waiting to happen."

Lena stared. "We started this together. I'm not just here to rock babies and stay quiet when it's convenient. I'm the better negotiator. Let me handle it."

"That was before. Now, I lead. You follow." The words were final.

Lena tried to stand her ground, trembling with the need to shout something back and remind Mira that she wasn't just a shadow in her wake, but Mira had already turned away. She swallowed the words and turned toward the stairs, each step a reluctant surrender. Halfway down, she paused and looked back. From that angle, everything had shrunk. Mira was at the prow, hair snapping like a banner, with the ship stretched beneath her like a creature poised to strike. She looked like a captain carved from mahogany - glorious, and utterly alone. This wasn't how it was meant to be. They used to plan side by side, whispering into the dark, trading warmth and ideas. Now Mira stood crowned in command, and Lena couldn't even say her name without triggering something dark.

I don't need your help.

Mira believed that. Lena didn't. She leaned against the wall, arms crossed tight. Mira didn't need someone to obey her, she needed someone to argue, but the more Lena tried, the further Mira ran.

On deck, the wind caught the sails in sharp little tugs. The ship strained forward, eager. The other vessel closed in. Lena squeezed her eyes shut, and for a moment she felt herself standing elsewhere. On ships she'd never seen, in places that didn't exist. Sand under her feet. Rain on stone. A dozen skies, familiar and wrong. Then it was gone.

When she opened her eyes. Mira stood at the ready, sword at her side, eyes full of storm. The other ship loomed closer, and from her hidden perch on the narrow stairs, Lena pressed herself into the shadows. The cannon fired with a crack that split the air wide open. Lena flinched, heart lurching. Mira hadn't even reached for the controls. The ship had decided on its own.

"Board them," Mira snapped, eyes fixed on the enemy ship bearing down on them. "Now."

Erik hesitated at the rail, rope in hand. "Captain, they have weapons. If we get closer, they'll fire."

"Do you doubt me?" Her voice cracked like thunder.

He winced. "No, Captain. I just - "

"Then act like it." Her hand fell to her sword, and Lena thought she might draw it on him. Erik threw the rope. "Hesitation gets people killed," Mira muttered to whatever gods might be listening. The crew moved into action. They surged forward, grappling hooks soared, iron teeth catching the enemy ship's hull. One found purchase, then another. Wood groaned as the lines snapped taut and the two ships collided. The other ship didn't go quietly. A flash burst from its mid-deck, followed by a hiss and a blast. Their ship rocked as something scorched its hull, but the damage held. Another flare streaked for the sails, veering wide at the last moment, as if the wind had shifted just in time.

Mira didn't flinch. "Bridge secured?"

"Locked!" someone shouted.

"Then go."

The crew charged. Steel met steel and screams tangled with the clash of blades. Mira's crew cut through the enemy, fast, focused, driven by her fury. Or was it fear? All the while, she stood watch like a crazed queen. At last someone raised the white flag.

When it was over. Mira strode across the sky bridge, unhurried. The enemy captain waited on the far side, breathless. He raised both hands high, then lowered one in a gesture of surrender. Slowly, he extended it to Mira with an open palm, head bowed.

"Please," he said. "I yield."

Mira looked at the hand, then his eyes, and smiled. She grabbed the front of his coat and shoved, sending him tumbling backward into the sky, his scream rising before the wind swallowed it whole. Without a word, she turned and walked back across the sky bridge, boots ringing against the metal.

Lena slid down onto the steps, breath shallow. Her hands trembled as she pressed them to her face, the pounding in her ears drowning out the sounds above as Mira's crew stripped the air-dweller ship bare. *What are we becoming?* The thought landed too late, but there was no room for grief. Not yet. She didn't know how long she sat there before her body rose without asking, and headed down the corridor. The door to Mira's cabin hung half-open. She stopped short. Inside, Derrick sat cross-legged on the floor, rocking Skye gently. His expression was too old for his face, his voice soft and rhythmic.

"What are you saying?" Lena asked.

"A prayer," he murmured, eyes still on the baby. "Like the ones Kashan used to say before a storm. What happened?"

Lena hesitated, then forced a smile. It felt brittle. "Nothing you need to worry about."

She crouched, lowering herself to his level. "Everything's going to be fine," she lied.

Skye whimpered, her eyelids fluttering. Her gaze flicked past Lena toward the sound of Mira's voice, sharp on the wind outside. The baby flinched and her fingers curled tighter in Derrick's shirt. Even the baby could feel the storm that was coming.

Derrick rubbed her back in small circles. "I promise to always keep her safe," he whispered. The words hit like a punch and for a heartbeat, Lena didn't see Derrick at all, only the captain Mira had shoved.

This is too much for him. Without thinking, she reached for Derrick, pulling him into a hug. He stiffened, but then he folded into her. "You don't have to hold this by yourself," she said. "I'll keep you safe. Both of you. I promise." She didn't know how. The words felt impossible, but she meant it. *They can't see this,* she thought as she pulled back, brushing a curl from his forehead. *They can't grow up thinking this is normal. I won't let them.*

Derrick nodded, it wasn't fair for someone so young to be that steady, Lena squeezed his hand before rising then turned to the door. Above, Mira was still carving her path forward through cloud and ruin, but here, in this quiet space, Lena made her own vow.

I won't let them lose themselves to this. Not while I still have breath.

CHAPTER 8

The village appeared through the porthole, familiar and wrong all at once. It should have felt comforting. It had the same patchwork roofs and crooked palisade she remembered, but something about it felt...off. Lena pressed her forehead to the glass. She'd only been gone a few months, but the place felt smaller.

She hadn't slept well since returning to her own cabin. Mira's pacing had started again, restless loops above deck. Some nights, it was a mug crashing against the wall. Other times - yelling. Lena never asked, and Mira never offered.

She'd suggested letting Skye sleep in her quarters instead. Mira had refused. The child stayed with her and that was final. Lena supposed it was a good sign that Mira's anger had never touched the baby. If anything, Skye was the last thread keeping her from unraveling, but even that was fraying. Lena saw it in the clenched jaw, and the silence that stretched too long.

They had attacked two more ships since that first raid. Each one faster, more brutal. No warnings. The Raven struck, stripped, and left the others limping away. At least Mira hadn't killed anyone else. The hold was overflowing with food, water, and fuel. It was more than the village could use in a year. Maybe two.

Still, Mira counted. "It's not enough," she'd muttered one night, fingers skimming the ledger.

Lena had glanced over the numbers. "Mira, this could last for years."

"Years are nothing," Mira replied, eyes dark. "I'm thinking bigger." After the last raid, she stood at the helm. "This will keep us more than afloat," she'd said. "It's time we returned home."

***

The Raven hovered above their village now, laden with stolen bounty.

Lena stepped back from the porthole and pushed open the door and moved toward the deck. Light hit her face as she stepped outside. She gripped a rail as the village drew closer. The crew worked around her, checking lines, readying descent. No one smiled.

At the prow, Mira stood like a blade. Hair loose in the wind, eyes rimmed dark. She didn't scan the village like someone returning home, she watched it like prey. "Everything ready?" she called over her shoulder. One deckhand nodded, his gaze dropping. Lena didn't blame him. Few people could meet The Raven's eyes now and walk away feeling whole.

The ship settled onto the cracked earth, its shadow stretched long across the village, darkening the dirt paths and sagging rooftops. The crew moved with practiced rhythm, unloading crates of food, barrels of water, and rolls of dyed fabric that looked out of place against the village's faded gray. Still, people gathered. Faces lit not with joy, exactly, but something close. Relief, maybe.

Lena stood beside Mira as they looked down at the scene. The villagers' murmurs stirred something in her, but it wasn't pride. The place looked the same, rooflines she'd memorized as a child, the same weather-beaten fence, but it no longer felt like hers.

Kashan reached them first. She'd braced for his skepticism, but his eyes swept over the supplies with barely restrained wonder. "This will keep us fed for months," he said, already calculating. "Maybe a year."

Not a single question. Not even *where did this come from?* "You're welcome," Mira said, her tone flat.

Kashan blinked, then summoned a too-wide smile. "Oh, Mira, child. You know I'm grateful. I'm sorry. I should've said that first. This was your idea, yours and Lena's, and it's been... fruitful."

"It has," she said, eyes never leaving the crew.

Elin followed behind, more measured. Where Kashan's energy vibrated with gratitude, Elin's presence felt like a balm. Her eyes lingered on Mira with a kind of quiet searching, as if trying to find the girl she'd once known inside this steel-wrapped version. "And Derrick?" she asked, eyes on the ship. "And the child?"

As if summoned, Derrick appeared at the top of the gang-plank, Skye swaddled tight against his chest. His steps were careful, and his small hands gripped the railing with caution. He didn't falter. Lena watched his every step, heart tight. He looked older, but he was still just a boy. Raised mostly by Kashan and Elin, Derrick now seemed to stand halfway between the child they remembered and something not quite grown. He reached the bottom of the ramp and paused, scanning the crowd until his eyes found Elin. His face softened as he stepped forward and wrapped his arms around her, careful not to disturb Skye in the sling.

"You've grown," Elin said, pulling him close. "And you're carrying quite the responsibility."

Derrick straightened, his voice small but steady. "I can handle it."

Lena felt a smile tug at her mouth. The moment was tender, but the knot inside her chest only tightened. Something in the air hummed wrong. The village, the crates, even the wind, all felt stretched, like something would give.

That night, the crew scattered across the village, returning to families or bedding down in corners that offered quiet. Privacy was rare aboard the ship, and some took the chance to sleep alone. A few untouched cabins remained near the stern, part of Mira's long-standing plan. *For families,* she had said, but Lena had her doubts. They felt less like gifts and more like rewards, handed out to those who earned Mira's favor.

Skye already had one waiting for when she was older. A room of her own, something Lena had never known. Ultimately, the ship belonged to Skye in a way it didn't to anyone else.

It was where she came from. Lena shoved the thought aside. In their months of travel, no one had spoken of a lost infant. And with Mira's way: hit hard, grab what was useful, vanish. Maybe no one ever would. Lena shook the thought away. Tonight wasn't for Skye.

For the first time in a week, Lena was in Mira's cabin. Derrick and Skye were both at Kashan's. Mira's touch was warm and steady, fingers at Lena's hip. It reminded her why she was here at all. Lena leaned in, brushing her mouth against Mira's, fingers sliding into dark hair, and pulling her close. Mira answered with intensity, mouth insistent. They clung to each other like the world might break apart without warning. For a moment, there was only the heat between them. Tangled limbs, quiet gasps, the hush of sheets. But the tension never fully left. Even as Lena pressed closer, tried to drown in the press of Mira's body, it stayed. Mira shifted back, settling against the bedframe. The quiet returned.

"This," Lena said. "It's beautiful. But it won't last."

Mira turned, one brow raised, eyes unreadable. "What's that supposed to mean?"

Lena drew her knees to her chest. "The cheering, the smiles, the full bellies. It's just a bandage. You know it. This won't hold."

Mira's jaw tightened. "It's enough for today."

"It's not." Lena's voice caught frustration creeping in like a tide. "You feel it too. How long before it breaks? Before a ship fires first? Before we take too much and leave someone else starving?"

"So what then? We let our people go hungry? Wait around to be picked off by the ship we meet? Just *hope* the world grows a conscience?"

"There's a difference between surviving and becoming what we hate." Lena's words rushed out. "We could talk to them. Just once. Ask. *Find out where Skye came from.* For gods' sake, Mira, we're gutting lives and vanishing before they even know who we are."

Mira's expression didn't change, but something flickered behind her eyes. "And what would you feel if you were in my place? Sitting in this bed, deciding who eats and who gets left behind? Don't lecture me like it's simple."

Lena leaned forward. "It's not simple. But it's ours. Or it *should be.* It's supposed to be shared." She reached out, but Mira had already stood, turning away.

"Maybe you should go back to your cabin," Mira didn't look back. "I think we've talked enough."

Lena stood, and her feet were cold on the floor. She paused at the door, hoping, but Mira was already staring out the window, unreachable.

***

Lena woke to the sound of footsteps and low voices drifting through the hull. She stretched, blinked against the morning light, and pushed herself upright. Padding to the deck, she rubbed the sleep from her eyes and then stopped cold.

Villagers and crew clustered around the ship like ants over a carcass. Sheets of dark metal were being fitted over the old hull, swallowing the last glimmers of gold. Even the figurehead was changing, its curved gull's wings hammered flat, reshaped into something sharper. Her breath caught. The ship had never quite felt like it belonged to them. Now, it looked like it belonged to Mira. Like it *was* Mira.

Mira moved among them, barking orders, rallying cheers. Her voice struck the air like iron on stone. And the people followed with no hesitation. Whatever the ship had once been, it wasn't a symbol of hope anymore. It was a warning. The golden shine was gone, buried beneath shadows. Mira's hands were streaked with soot, the black rim around her eyes like war paint. Each layer made her less human. Lena watched, numb, as Mira climbed onto a crate and faced the crowd.

"From this day on," she called, "I am The Raven. We will take what we need from the sky, and they will remember us."

The crowd erupted. This wasn't the girl she used to hold in the quiet hours, the one who once whispered fears in the dark. This was someone who believed she was owed the sky.

Lena moved through the crowd to Mira and whispered, "Are you sure this is the path? There must be a way that gives peace to all."

"The air-dwellers gave us nothing," she whispered to Lena, then louder to all. "We take. We survive. That's all that matters now."

The cheers swelled again. Mira wasn't just leading them, she was becoming something else. Whatever path she was carving through the clouds, she wasn't making space for Lena to walk beside her.

CHAPTER 9

The Raven's mission had shifted. She was no longer content with opportunistic raids. This was not merely survival, it was expansion. Mira had transformed their efforts into a campaign of dominion, her fleet growing stronger, and her reputation grew. The air-dwellers whispered her name in fear now.

They were currently docked in a village on the ground. Lena supervised as the crew unloaded their spoils. Villagers, worn down from years of struggle, watched with awe. Gazes flickered between The Raven and the crates of stolen goods. Hands trembled when they made their offerings, with shoulders hunched as if bracing for unseen consequences. They murmured their thanks, but voices lacked warmth, only relief that they had bought another day of safety.

In the months that had passed, tribute became the price for The Raven's protection. It was the symbol of Mira's promise to redistribute wealth and free enslaved settlements. Mira made sure the villagers never forgot who held the power. "They give tribute, we give protection," she had told Lena. *Simple.*

But now, Lena saw the quiet desperation in the people's eyes. This wasn't an exchange, it was submission. The Raven was just another ship carrying air dwellers. The worst part? Mira saw it too. She just didn't care.

Lena's stomach twisted with disgust as the first villager stepped forward, clutching their offering with a look of resignation. The sight was too much. She turned on her heel and walked away, retreating to her quarters and slamming the door behind her. She wanted to run. But she couldn't. Not because of Mira. Not anymore, but because of Skye and Derrick. If she left, who would remind them what the world was supposed to be?

Hours later, once she was certain everyone had returned to the ship, Lena made her way to Mira's cabin. She passed through the halls; she heard Derrick speaking with one of the crew. His voice had lost its childish softness.

"They'll give what they can, and if they don't, we take it." She paused in the corridor, barely daring to breathe. That voice belonged to a child who once sang lullabies to a girl who might save the world.

A younger crew member chuckled. "Kid's not wrong."

"Yeah," Derrick replied. "Raven says no one gives you anything for free."

Lena wanted to throw up. The words weren't even Mira's, but her lessons had nested in his mouth like seeds in dry earth. And now they were blooming. He was watching and learning all the wrong things.

As she neared Mira's cabin, a muffled voice seeped through the door. Then came Mira's laughter freezing Lena in her tracks.

She hadn't heard Mira laugh like that in months. She raised her hand to knock, but the laughter stopped, and a series of rustling sounds caught her attention. Dread prickled at her skin and with a sharp inhale, she pushed the door open. The sight hit her like a blow. Clothes lay in a heap on the floor, and the bed was a mess of tangled sheets and rumpled blankets.

Mira was straddling a man, her head thrown back, the dark paint beneath her eyes smudged and running. Her hands pressed against his chest, his sun-browned skin slick with sweat. His arms curled around her waist, drawing her in with each slow, grinding movement.

The room was hot, every detail searing itself into Lena's brain.

"Mira," she whispered.

Mira turned her head, her eyes locking onto Lena. She leaned back and slid off the man. Then rose to her feet and crossed her arms over her chest.

"Leave us," Mira said to the man.

He hesitated, and for a moment, lingered. Mira's glare shifted to him, and that was enough. Muttering something under his breath, he bent to retrieve his clothes. He avoided Lena's eyes as he brushed past her, the scent of sweat and sex trailing in his wake. The door clicked shut behind him, leaving the two women alone.

Mira met her gaze without shame. "You disapprove." It wasn't a question.

"You think this is different from what Captain Hawthorn did to you?" Lena's voice wavered.

Mira stiffened. For a moment, Lena thought she saw something crack in her. Then it was gone.

"They offer," Mira said coldly. "I accept." She turned back to Lena, her arms still crossed, her jaw set like stone. "Was there something you needed?"

Lena's hands trembled at her sides. Her eyes flicked to Mira. The woman before her wasn't the one she had fallen in love with. This was The Raven. Lena stared, her chest tight. "Mira, he's a person, not a sack of grain."

"He was not forced." Mira turned away, picking up a small compact and dabbing at the paint beneath her eyes, as if the conversation was nothing more than a passing inconvenience. "They know what's at stake. They know we protect them."

"And you're okay with this? Taking what they offer, like it doesn't matter?" Lena's voice cracked, her anger spilling over. "How is this any different from what Captain Hawthorn did to you?"

Mira froze mid-motion, the brush hovering just above her cheek. She turned to face Lena, her expression darkening. "That," Mira said, her voice deadly, "is not the same."

"It isn't?" Lena pressed. "He took what he wanted because he had power over you. He made you feel like you were nothing. And now you're doing the same, Mira. Don't you see that?"

"Enough," Mira snapped. Her eyes burned with an intensity that made Lena flinch, but she didn't back down.

"Mira, please," Lena said, her voice shook. "This isn't you. This isn't who you are."

Mira turned away. "Leave."

For a long time, she just watched. Mira didn't move, her focus locked on her reflection as she dabbed at the smudged paint beneath her eyes. Silence stretched between them, wide and aching, until it felt like a chasm. With a breath caught in her chest, Lena hesitated. The woman before her was vanishing behind armor and war paint. As she turned to go, a sound broke the quiet and instinct pulled her back. In Mira's grip, the compact mirror shook. White-knuckled and taut, her hand held it like a lifeline. Her expression remained a mask, but the tremble betrayed what the rest of her refused to admit.

Swallowing the lump in her throat, Lena stepped out of the cabin. Behind her, the wind let out a mournful cry, a dirge for something already lost. Whatever Mira was becoming, Lena couldn't follow. The corridor outside felt colder, though the air hadn't changed. The sound of her boots echoed on the wooden boards as she moved, not sure where she was going. Her hands still trembled. Mira's voice, her face, the indifference, all looped through her mind. She had known things were getting worse, but she hadn't realized just how far the gap had grown. Not until now. She reached her cabin and closed the door quietly behind her. There was no crying. Just silence. In that silence, she felt something shift and, once something shifts, it's only a matter of time.

One thing was certain: Skye couldn't be lost in the storm. If Mira had become The Raven, then Lena would have to be The Owl, wise and clear-eyed, holding fast to the light. Where The Raven thrived in darkness, Lena would fight to ensure neither the skies nor the earth were consumed by it.

Her gaze drifted to the horizon, where storm clouds loomed. The wind shifted again, carrying the sour scent of ozone. A storm was brewing, yes, but it wasn't just in the clouds. It crackled in the wood of the deck, hummed beneath the ship's feet. Lena closed her eyes. Somewhere out there, the sky remembered what it meant to fall. Somewhere, the earth whispered its own truths; quiet, ancient things that Mira had stopped listening to.

INTERLUDE

There are only a few clouds in the sky. Wispy cirrus ones, like the feathers of the birds that used to fill the skies. I stare at them through the window, knowing it has to be today. No longer will I sit in this gilded cage, the so-called princess of a prophecy that will never come to be. I will fly free, and they will never find me.

Last night, I wrote two letters. One to my mother, The Raven, who only sees me as a tool. It was cold and calculating, just like her. I thought about telling the truth, exposing everything, but Lena was right, hope is all they have left. The second letter was for Lena, The Owl. She is the one who truly raised me, the one who will miss me. She deserves my forgiveness.

I pull the apparatus from my mahogany wardrobe, the leather straps creaking as I loop them over my arms. The wings are lined with hundreds of feathers I've collected over the years, mostly for aesthetics, but they make me feel like I belong somewhere. Somewhere out there.

Derrick is outside my door, like always. He's my shadow, part guard, part spy, and maybe part something else. He's too loyal to my mother and too kind to say no to her orders. I'm not sure if he even knows which part of him is real.

When I step out, his gaze flickers to me and away just as quickly, like I'm something dangerous to look at for too long. He's taller now, with broad shoulders that make him seem older than twenty. But his eyes - those are still the eyes of the boy who used to sit with me by candlelight, telling me stories he probably made up on the spot.

"What are you wearing?" he asks, concerned.

I don't answer. I walk past him, my wings brushing his arm as I head toward the stern of the ship.

He follows, his footsteps growing more frantic when I climb onto the rim. "Skye!" he shouts. "Get down! You're going to fall!"

I pause, just for a moment, long enough to feel his worry. Guilt coils in my chest. I know what this will cost him. He'll face my mother's wrath, and he might not survive it. But that's out of my hands now. I can only hope Lena will protect him.

The warmth of the sun creeps over my face, and I spread my wings wide. There is a flicker of something strange, and just for an instant, I see myself below. I wonder what Derrick sees when he looks at me now, the girl he once cared for or the selfish, reckless creature I've become.

I leap into the air.

The wings jolt as they catch the updraft, and I don't look back. I never look back. I only look forward, carried by the gale pulling me away. I angle my wings, adjusting for the wind, but the sky ripples just enough that my body feels out of place, and I'm only just catching up to where I was supposed to be.

Then I plummet. The ground is too close. I brace for impact. My mind screams to adjust, to twist, and the world shatters.

PART 2

Gemini

WOLF GROVE MEDIA, LLC

CHAPTER 10

THE OWL

I shut my eyes as the warmth of the sun creeps over my face, and I leap into the air. My wings jolt as they catch the updraft, and I do not look back, only forward, carried by the gale pulling me away. Lately, dreams have been more tactile. Like memory, but wrong. I wake with the feeling of wind behind my ribs, as if wings I don't have have just folded themselves shut.

When I open my eyes, I'm still on the ground, my hands buried in my pockets as the sea breeze curls around me. It's just a dream. A memory, maybe. Or perhaps it's something deeper, buried so far inside me that it feels like instinct. The moment fades, leaving me grounded.

Above, a great black-backed gull glides, its wings spread wide, riding the same air that brushes my cheeks. I envy how it commands the sky, unbound and untouchable. The largest of its kind, it owns the space it inhabits. It is a creature of contrasts with its white crown and dark wings slicing through the brilliant light of morning. Behind my eyes, restless birds beat their wings, longing to break free, yet I'm tethered to the earth, like the mist clinging to the tide, unable to rise above it.

My life feels caught in transition, suspended between what it was and what it's trying to become. I walk to work with my head down, the pavement under my feet uneven. The gull cries above in a sharp, commanding call that echoes in the quiet streets. It doesn't care if anyone is listening. Sometimes I imagine what it would feel like to live with that kind of certainty, to cut through the world like it belongs to me.

Prescott Park is empty now, but by late morning, it will hum with life. Young people in flowing skirts and tie-dye shirts will lounge in or outside cafes steeped in the scent of espresso and burnt toast, their laughter rising like smoke from clove cigarettes. They always seem to hold some quiet secret, an effortless way of belonging that the rest of us don't understand. Sometimes, I watch them and wonder what it feels like to live so freely, to walk through the world as if your skin fits.

At the diner, the morning crowd swells. Strangers are leaning over cups of coffee, staring at their phones. I weave between tables, refilling mugs and remembering orders. If I disappeared right now, I doubt anyone would look up long enough to notice.

Nothing about me ever seems to stick. I'm unremarkable, unmemorable like beige wallpaper in a world of vivid murals. I'm the kind of person who can sit next to you for hours, and you'll still jump when I finally speak. If the universe had an opinion about me, it would be a shrug.

Time slides sideways sometimes. One moment I reach for something and find it already in my hand. Conversations I don't remember answering continue like I've been there all along. The clock on the wall flickers in my peripheral vision. Ten minutes have passed, but I swear it was only a blink. I've started to wonder if time is skipping for everyone or just for me.

I keep hoping that someday things will change and eventually, I will grow into myself. Here I am, an adult, still reminding people of my name only for them to forget it. Now, when I come up in conversation, it's usually, "Oh! She's the Hartwell kid, right?" as if "Skye" is just a label in my parents' filing cabinet instead of my own name, myself.

My childhood was odd, no way around it. Around thirteen, I woke up one day with no memory of who I was or where I'd come from. No head injury, no fever, no dramatic brush with death to explain it. One moment I was a person with a past, and the next, nothing. Just a blank slate where my life before should have been.

That was the story, anyway. The doctors called it retrograde amnesia, but they couldn't tell me much else. I was found lying on the beach near Wallis Sands, my clothes damp, sand clinging to my skin. No one came forward to claim me, and I had nothing. No ID, no name, just the clothes on my back and a strange pendant they found with me.

You'd think something like that would make me unforgettable. Maybe a curiosity, a medical mystery that experts would scramble to unravel. But it didn't. After a few weeks in the system, the world carried on. And I was just... there.

That's when the Hartwells found me.

I know I exist; there are photos to prove it. Me and Mom at the beach, my first Christmas with Dad handing me a ridiculously oversized stocking, a blurry snapshot of us laughing over a board game. There's even one of me in a cap and gown at eighth-grade graduation, their faces glowing with pride.

But those pictures feel like fragments from someone else's life. I can say, "That's us," but the memories don't feel like mine. And no one ever says, "Remember when?" about them. Not because they've forgotten, but because they are afraid I will.

They don't want to rub in the fact that nothing before thirteen exists for me. Maybe they think it's kinder that way, letting those years rest instead of reminding me I've lost something. Or maybe they're afraid to bring it up, like talking about it might tempt the amnesia back, wiping out everything we've built since.

I try not to think about it, but ignoring it doesn't make it hurt less. It just makes the silence louder.

They've given me so much but sometimes it feels like I'm holding on to it all by a thread. Like my life is borrowed, and I'm just waiting for the day the thread snaps.

I love them for trying so hard to make me whole, even if I can't shake the fear that I'll never really belong.

Since then, my memory's been sharp. Almost too sharp. It's like my brain's been working overtime to make up for what it lost. I memorize song lyrics after a single listen, catch details others miss. My mind feels like a restless machine, cataloging moments before they can slip away. I absorb these tiny details like they might prove something about me, but I don't know what. It's strange, isn't it? How I can memorize other people's lives, but my own past is just a locked room with no key.

Inside, I'm a kaleidoscope of feelings, colors, and sounds. I am a wild, brilliant mix of everything that makes me. I am beautiful. Amazing, even. None of that translates. What I am on the inside comes out muted, dull, gray. All that vibrance gets tangled up somewhere between my mind and my words, lost in translation.

Here, under the fluorescent lights of Sunshine Diner, that translation glitch is on display for anyone who bothers to look (not that anyone does). I'm invisible as ever, just a pair of hands topping off mugs and memorizing orders, blending into the hum of customers and coffee cups. They see the waitress who brings their order, but never me.

Mr. Green sits in his usual corner booth, reading an honest-to-goodness newspaper. I walk over, coffee pot in hand, and pause just long enough for him to acknowledge me. He never does.

"Refill?" I ask anyway. My voice comes out soft. Not timid, just... too easy to ignore.

He places a hand over his cup, and doesn't look up.

Before I can turn away, Annie breezes past me. "Paul!" she chirps, and just like that, his whole posture changes. His face lifts, and a genuine smile unfolds. She takes the pot from my hands like I was never there, topping off his cup.

"Thanks, dear," he says, warm as toast.

I let my feet carry me back behind the counter. No one is trying to be cruel, I remind myself. It's just how people see me. Or don't.

I've been working at Sunshine's for almost a year now, ever since I dropped out of college. I keep saying I'll go back to school someday, but every time I think about it, the idea slips through my fingers. Nothing there grabs me. My mom keeps pushing, telling me I should go, that she'll pay for it. She wants me to be something important. Something that'll make her look good.

The thought of those classrooms makes me feel like I'm suffocating, like the walls are crowding in and the windows only open a crack. Everyone with their shiny laptops and polished lives, so sure of where they're going. Meanwhile, I was there trying to feel like I belonged, like I was more than just a name and a number.

My freshman year, I was surrounded by people, like maybe I'd cracked the code on being seen. Parties, hiking, concerts - you name it, I was there. It always felt like I was trying too hard. I drank too much, smoked way too much, anything to build up the courage to just be there. And it worked. People laughed, cheered, even hugged me goodbye at the end of the night. But I was never the one people called first, never the friend anyone texted to check in. I had to claw my way into every single interaction, fighting for space in my own friendships.

The memory surfaced, blurring the present for just a moment. I could still hear the lazy trickle of the river, sunlight glinting on its surface as I sat cross-legged on the rocks. Laughter drifted up around me, mingled with the acrid scent of pot and the hum of summer. Someone leaned in with a grin, tossing out a joke that was more mean-spirited than funny. The group erupted in laughter, and I did too. It was a reflex I'd perfected, even when it didn't reach my eyes.

Inside, I felt the familiar tug of something else. The ache to be somewhere else, seeing the world, diving into discussions that set my mind ablaze. That's what I wanted. Yet I stayed by the river, laughing at jokes I didn't like and letting the minutes slip away, afraid of what would happen if I stopped showing up. I knew too well that absence meant silence, messages drying up, friends moving on, and the realization that if I wasn't there, I'd simply be forgotten.

The memory faded, leaving a bitter aftertaste. It was exhausting, always pretending. I couldn't keep up the act and left after one semester. I had torn myself apart trying to be the person everyone else seemed to see.

So here I am. I don't have to try to be anything or anyone. Usually, I pick up the lunch shift, too, but no one's called in sick today, so I'm off at eleven. I lean against the counter, doodling an owl on my order pad as I wait for my shift to end.

The clang of dishes jolts me back. "Skye, are you clocking out soon?" Annie's voice pulls me into the present.

I glance at the time and realize I've been standing here, lost in thought, for far too long. The lunch crowd is growing. I pull my apron off and toss it into the laundry bin. "Yeah," I call back. "I'm heading out now."

The bell above the door jingles as I step into the sunlight, the breeze brushing my face like a quiet reminder of everything I've been holding back. For a moment, I close my eyes and breathe in the salt-tinged air. There's this feeling in my bones lately, like my body wants to be somewhere else before my mind catches up, and if I don't figure out where I'm going soon, I might just start walking and never stop.

The sun is high when I get home and I push open the front door. I expect the familiar quiet, the echo of an empty house filled with perfectly placed decor and the faint scent of my mom's expensive candles. Instead, I'm greeted by the clink of dishes and the sound of classical music floating from the kitchen.

Mom? Home at noon? That's not typical. Mom, the force behind Hartwell Solutions, doesn't do lunch breaks unless it involves networking over appetizers.

I step inside and glance at the family photos lined up on the hallway shelf. They're a mix of Mom and Dad's polished, professional lives and the small moments they've tried to capture with me. Mom at galas or award ceremonies, always poised and smiling in her tailored dresses. Next to that is Dad in his white coat at the hospital, standing with his arm around a group of grinning residents.

Then there are the ones with all three of us: me in Mickey ears at Disney World, standing stiffly between Mom and Dad. me and Dad at some street festival, or sitting between them on the couch with popcorn bowls balanced precariously on our laps. They try so hard to make it look seamless. Like we've always been this way. Sometimes, when I pass too quickly, my reflection doesn't follow. Just for a split second, I'll catch the hallway empty of pictures even though I'm right there.

There's also the gap they don't talk about. No baby pictures of me and no awkward school photos from before eighth grade. Nothing to prove I existed before they found me. It's better that way, Mom always says. "Why dwell on what you don't remember when you've got so much ahead of you?"

Dad says less about it, but I've caught the way his smile falters when I bring up my past - or lack of one. Like he's afraid it might disappear all over again if we talk about it too much.

"Skye, is that you?" My attention snaps back to the present. Mom's commanding tone cuts through the quiet. It's the kind of voice that never needs to be raised to be heard.

"Yeah, it's me," I answer, making my way to the kitchen. She's there, perched on a barstool with a salad in front of her and her phone angled precariously on the counter. She's in full CEO attire - suit jacket and heels that look more sculpted than worn.

"You're home early," she says with that underlying hint of judgment that always makes me feel like she's sizing up a quarterly report. "No lunch shift today?"

"Nope. They didn't need me." I grab a glass from the cabinet and fill it with water, focusing on small, familiar actions.

She nods, stabbing at her salad. "Well, it's good you have some time to yourself. "You should use this time to think about going back to school," she says, the same way someone might remind you to get your oil changed. My mother doesn't ask about my dreams, my wants. She just maps out a version of me that fits inside her world.

"I'll think about it," I say, because it's easier than explaining the way college made me feel like I was suffocating. For just a second, I think she might say something else, but then her phone buzzes, and just like that, I am an afterthought again.

"I won't be long," she says, standing up and tossing the rest of her salad into the trash. "Just stopping in before my next meeting. You know how it is."

"Yeah," I murmur as she grabs her bag and breezes past me. The air shifts when she leaves, taking her energy with it. The house feels bigger, emptier, like a theater after the curtains go down and the audience leaves.

I take my water upstairs, footsteps muffled by the runner carpet. My room is the one place that hasn't changed. The lavender paint from high school still clings to the walls and glow-in-the-dark stars hang on like relics. I change into comfortable clothes, tugging a hoodie over my head as I sink into my bed.

The quiet presses in, but at least it's my quiet. I stretch out on the bed, letting my limbs sink into the worn comforter as my eyelids grow heavy. Maybe just a quick nap. The afternoon sun filters through the blinds, warm and dappled, casting patterns that move across the walls. I let my eyes close, willing the familiar haze to take over.

Sleep is where I slip out of my skin, where the dull edges of the day dissolve into something more. Dreams are greedy, hoarding their secrets, letting me hold only the impressions - bright as polished stones - that linger long after waking. The world softens around me, hushed as if it's holding its breath, waiting for something strange and beautiful to step out.

A breeze, cool and tinged with the metallic scent of storms, whispers over my face. It doesn't belong here, not in my sun-warmed room. I frown, the oddness brushing the edge of awareness. Behind my closed eyes, shapes unfurl - shadowed and luminous, merging in a dance I can't quite follow. The outline of a place emerges, tangled in twilight. Mist twines through the scene, silver threads around splintered bits of forgotten things:

the curve of an old chair leg, a cog from some long-dead clock, rusted trinkets that glint mournfully. My chest tightens.

I reach out, desperate to touch this half-formed world, but the vision coils away, the mist swallowing it. The room's reality pushes back, warm and unmoving, a blanket that traps instead of comforts. But that flicker of connection, like a phantom hand on my shoulder, remains. A whisper - half-hope, half-dare - clings to me, a promise that I can't quite hear but feel down to my bones.

Somewhere in that space, a shape moves, too purposeful to be a trick of my mind. The thought that I know this place flickers in and out like an unsteady flame, leaving me breathless.

I let go, sinking into the pull of sleep. The weight of the day fades, and an exhilarating lightness rises in its place. Here, I am not beige wallpaper or a barely there outline. Here, I am bright and bold, a creature that runs through realms unknown. The air shifts, and somewhere in the distance, a voice calls my name, not the way someone calls across a street, but the way a story calls to its beginning. It wraps around me like a thread tugging at my ribs, pulling tighter. I jolt awake with the name still echoing, not sure if it was mine or someone else's. But I know one thing for sure.

I have to go. I just don't know where yet.

CHAPTER II

The Raven

I clamp my eyes shut, bracing against the shrieking wind as vapors coil around my cheeks. A crack tears through the air as The Raven's sails snap open. Beneath my feet, I can feel the engine vibrating and I force my eyes open just in time to see the ship surge forward.

I've never seen a real bird, only the ones in books. Still, I collect their feathers. The Raven mimics their flight, but it feels unnatural. Much like my life. Sometimes, when I sleep, I see birds I've never known. White gulls with wings stretched wide, crying over a sea I've never seen. I wake with the taste of salt on my tongue and the sound of waves I've never heard.

I think... I think part of me remembers a place I've never been.

The Raven is an empire, built to carry my mother's will like a winged god. She commands the storm, bends men to their knees with a glance, speaks, and they listen. I am her legacy. The daughter of prophecy. The girl meant to inherit it all. But inherit what, exactly? A throne I cannot sit upon? A kingdom that is not mine to rule?

My mother is beautiful, wise, and adored. To the people, she can do no wrong. To me, she's a master of facades, sustaining her power with cruelty and cunning. I watch her at the helm, her obsidian hair whipping in the wind. The crew watches too, their eyes full of hunger. I hate that I want to be just like her. She wasn't always alone, Lena used to stand beside her. They used to speak with their eyes more than words. Now Lena keeps to the shadows.

I don't know what happened between them, but it broke something in my mother. Or maybe it revealed something that was already broken.

I spit in disgust and head toward my quarters. Derrick trails like a puppy at my heels. Nearby crew members pause just long enough to remind me they're watching. Do they see me at all, or only the captain's daughter?

"You can go," I say, waving Derrick off without looking. One of the deckhands pretends to adjust a rope but glances my way, expecting some sort of scene. "No one's going to bother me on this ship," I continue.

"But... but your mother said I'm your shield. How can I keep you safe if you keep sending me away?" He replies.

"Whatever. Stand outside my door all day if that makes you happy. Just leave me alone."

He hesitates, his mouth opening like he wants to argue. Then he closes it. "You used to tell me everything," he finally says.

I flinch, caught off guard. That's the trouble with people who've known you since childhood, they remember things you'd rather forget. "People change," I mutter and turn toward my cabin. His shoulders slump as he follows me. I should feel sorry for him, but if he had a spine, he wouldn't be on The Raven.

"Rift storm, dead ahead!" someone shouts from the lookout.

I whirl toward the horizon. Sure enough, streaks of green lightning fracture the sky, webbing through bruised clouds that churn like they're alive. As I stare, the green clouds shift, softening into puffy white masses. It shouldn't be possible. Not that fast anyway. A strange longing tugs from deep within. I grip the railing hard. For a moment, the world tilts and I swear I can feel the world breathing.

We tilt westward and Derrick reaches to steady me, and I swat his hand away. "I've grown up on this ship. I can catch my balance."

He steps back, hurt flickering across his face. My attitude is not fair to Derrick. He's been my shadow since before I could walk. I do care about him, but his hovering grates on my nerves. Mother's paranoia is to blame for that. She's convinced I'm a fragile bird with a broken wing.

When I reach my quarters, I slam the door shut. Inside, the engine's thrum wraps around me and I steady my breath. I slump against the wall and close my eyes. Derrick's out there, guarding my room, but who would be foolish enough to touch me? Part of me wishes someone would.

When I was thirteen, I jumped off The Raven. It wasn't rebellion; I was testing the limits of my cage. I had stood at the edge of the observation deck, staring down at the clouds. Beyond them lay the scorched earth. Mother always claimed healing the world was our mission, and reminded me that someday, I would be the one to do it.

The crew believed her, worshiping her as the person who would fix it all. Somewhere along the way, they forgot the prophecy that said I was supposed to be the one. Maybe she forgot, too.

I had long since accepted whatever was going to happen, until Lena told me it was all a lie. Then questions started to spin in my mind. If Mother truly cared about saving the earth below, why build her kingdom so far above their suffering? Lena was the first to say it. "She doesn't want to heal the land. She wants to rule what's left." She said it like someone delivering a truth that can't be unsaid. I never looked at Mother the same again.

Even if I wasn't really their savior, I wanted to know what it was like down there. I wanted to breathe the same air they did.

So I jumped.

It wasn't rebellion or even desperation. It was instinct. Like I knew I wasn't supposed to be here.

The fall was endless. Wind roared past my ears, my body slicing through the sky. The ship above shrank, a black shadow against the sun. Below, the clouds churned like a restless sea, something unseen waiting beneath them. For one beautiful moment, I thought I might become the sky itself.

When I woke up in my bed, my limbs were heavy and my head was pounding. The details of what happened afterward were hazy and my mother never spoke of it.. The fall should've killed me.

After that, I devoured every scrap of knowledge I could find about birds. They belong to both worlds, sky and earth, and they are free. My mother The Raven and Lena The Owl, wrapped in the myths they carried. But the more I read, the more I wondered. Were they free? Or were they just as caged as I was, draping themselves in feathers and calling it flight?

Power isn't always taken by force. Sometimes, it's a glance, a tilt of the head, a well-placed silence. I ease the door open, just a sliver. He's still there, lingering. I widen the gap, soften my gaze, let my lashes dip just so. I hate how easy it is. To slide into the shape she carved for me and make someone bend with nothing but a tilt of my head and a whisper.

I learned it from her. I don't want to be like her, but I don't know how to be anything else.

"Derrick..." My voice slips into something low and sweet. "I'm sorry. You didn't deserve that." His cheeks flush, and he blinks. I step closer, resting my hand on his shoulder, letting my fingers linger just a little longer than they need to. My lips part slightly as I meet his gaze. A faint tremor runs through him. Poor thing. "Forgive me?"

He melts. Just where I want him.

Derrick stands there, trapped between duty and desire, looking like he's about to either stammer an apology or backpedal out of the hallway. I smile, letting my hand slide from his shoulder to his wrist, and tug him across the threshold of my room.

"Come on." I give his wrist a reassuring squeeze as I guide him inside. "You're not scared, are you?"

His eyes widen. "No, I mean, of course not." But the tension in his arm says otherwise. He looks like he's wandered into a dragon's lair.

"Relax," I whisper.

Derrick swallows hard, his throat bobbing as his eyes flicker to the bed, then away. He's fighting it. I can see the tension in his shoulders. It should be easy. It is easy. I step closer, just enough to let the warmth of my skin brush his.

Then his muscles go rigid, and he takes a step back. "No." I blink. He shakes his head as if clearing a fog. "I can't." The words sound like they cost him something. "I won't."

The refusal lands like a slap. I let out a soft laugh, trying to cover the sharp edge in my voice. "My mother doesn't have to know."

"That's not the point." My pulse spikes. I don't understand. He wants this. I can see it in the way his fingers clench, in the way he won't quite meet my eyes. And yet, he won't.

"I'm not like that, Skye."

It's not the words themselves that sting, it's the certainty in his voice. The way he says it, as if he knows exactly what I'm doing. As if he has a choice. I tilt my head, letting the moment stretch between us.. His breath catches. I know how to play this game andI should be winning.

"My mother doesn't have to know," I murmur.

"That's not the point." His hands curl into fists, but when he looks at me, it isn't anger - it's disappointment. Something cold tightens in my chest. He wants this. I know he does. I can see it in the way he won't quite meet my eyes.

"I practically raised you," he whispers. "You're like a sister. I've spent half my life protecting you from her shadow, but lately... I don't know if I'm protecting you, or just holding onto the version of you I still understand." The words slam into me. A sister. Not a queen. Not a weapon. Not even a girl worth wanting.

I let my lips curl into a lazy smile, a practiced deflection. "Suit yourself."

He hesitates, like there's something else he wants to say. But then he leaves, and I am alone again. I used to believe Derrick would always be there, no matter what. But now I'm not so sure. It's not because he's pulling away, it's because I am. Maybe the worst part isn't that he said no, but that deep down, I wanted him to. My mask cracks. I don't know what unsettles me more, the fact that I failed, or the fact that I don't know how to be anything else. After collapsing into my bed, I pull the blankets tight, as if they could shut out the world.

I don't want to be her, I just don't know who to be.

The hum of The Raven's engines sings me a lullaby, and I allow myself to forget the world. A distant pulse, slow and steady. The ship shifts beneath me, and I am falling. The world softens, and the smell of metal and steam fade into something older. I'm at the edge of a cliff. The wind presses against my back, urging me forward. Below, a sea of clouds churn. Somewhere beneath them, the world still exists.

A whisper brushes my ear. "Jump." I know that voice.

Mother.

But when I glance over my shoulder, no one is there. I spread my arms, feeling the air coil beneath them. This is what I was meant for. For a moment, I fly. The wind roars past my ears, my stomach lurching with the drop.

Something is wrong.

A violent pull from the inside, like a thread unraveling from the fabric of my ribs. A split, not of flesh, but of something deeper that should not be touched. The feathers on my wings grow too heavy. Metal, not bone. Wire, not sinew. The air resists me, dragging me down like an unseen hand closing around my throat.

Something tears, and suddenly, I am weightless. No, I am nothing.

For a moment, I exist in two places at once, suspended and stretched between selves. The wind screams past me, but it doesn't feel real.

Then I rip apart.

There is no blood, no wound, no shattered bone. And yet, I know that I have been split. One part of me is still here, plummeting toward the clouds. The other is already gone.

The split echoes, not just in body, but in time and place. I see another version of me. Barefoot in a large room with strange tables, blinking in a too-bright world. I feel her ache, her confusion. I see the salt air through her eyes. She doesn't know she's me. Then the vision fractures. We're flung apart, she into light, I into storm. The scream catches in my throat, but it's not mine. It's hers. And she doesn't even know why she's crying.

CHAPTER 12

The Owl

Rhu and Violet have been in my life for as long as I can remember, though I'm not sure if "friendship" is the right word. We orbit each other, close enough to touch but never quite overlapping. They are the ones who stayed. Mostly.

I am the one who reaches out first, but they don't push me away, and try to connect with me in their own way. Rhu has her chaotic schemes and Violet, with her easy smiles. It's enough to keep me tethered. When I moved back in with my parents after dropping out of college, I threw myself into working long hours at the diner. The other hours, Rhu and Vi slid me right back into the fold.

Now, Rhu shows up unannounced. She pulls up in a cargo van that looks like it belongs in a low-budget horror movie. I can already tell she's got a plan. Of the two of them, Rhu is the one who keeps her cards close to her chest. She's deep, introspective, and has a low-burning anger I can't quite pin down. Vi is the opposite. Balanced and beautiful, she is the queen of our trio. Boys fall over themselves for her because she's sweet and docile.

But don't mistake her for soft. Vi's just as damaged; she just wears her mask better.

It's only Rhu tonight. My mom has never liked her. Rhu is the perfect mix of danger and innocence, and people don't know what to do with that.

"Want me to tell her you're not here?" my mom asks.

I roll my eyes. "No, Mom." I push past her and pull the door open, trying not to look surprised, but Rhu sees right through me.

"My new van," she says. "Wanna go for a ride?"

"Has that thing been inspected?" my mom calls from the living room. "Is it even safe to drive?"

Rhu smirks, opening her mouth to answer, but I jump in before she can. "I'm an adult, Mom. I'll be fine."

"If it breaks down, don't forget you've got AAA!" Mom fires back as I walk out of the door. "And your dad or I will come pick you up." She doesn't include Rhu in that offer.

Something flutters at the edge of my thoughts. Not real, but something in me knows there is danger coming. I've felt this pressure before, right before everything in my life changes. I almost back out, but the words catch in my throat like smoke.

We drive to the park around the corner, and Rhu is bouncing in her seat. Usually, she's the person who carries her intensity under the surface. But tonight, her excitement is spilling over. When she parks, we head straight for the bench we used to sit at in high school. It's tucked under a giant oak, the wood worn smooth. The air smells like damp grass and the sea.

"So, I have an idea," Rhu says as she flops onto the bench.

"Clearly."

"I think you, Vi, and I should get out of here. Explore the world, or at least the U.S. Just pack up and go. We can convert the van, throw in some beds, and see where the road takes us." The words hit me and a million feelings crash over me at once. It sounds perfect, beautiful, everything I've been craving without knowing it. Rhu and Vi are quicksilver at best, and Vi isn't even here to weigh in.

"It sounds good," I say, measuring my words. "But Vi's not here. What's she gonna say? I don't think she's just going to drop Aiden and leave."

Rhu grins, leaning forward. "What do you think she's doing right now?"

I raise an eyebrow. "Vi always has a boyfriend. When she breaks up with one, she already has the next lined up. She hates being alone."

"She won't be, she has us." Rhu's grin doesn't falter. "You work all the time, so you've probably got some cash saved up for gas, right?" Oh. That's why I'm part of this. Before I can respond, Rhu pushes on. "Vi and I have been putting some money aside. We've been talking about this for weeks. It's happening."

"What about..." My voice falters as nerves creep in. I scramble for an excuse, but nothing comes.

"Harvest Fire is next weekend," Rhu says. "I know you weren't planning on going this year, but it's the perfect dress rehearsal for our road trip!"

Harvest Fire. Part political rally, part Lammas celebration, and pure chaos.

People, even families with kids, show up. They come for lots of reasons: spirituality, activism, but let's be real, most just come to party.

"I don't know..." I blink hard. "I'm just... not sure."

Rhu's grin spreads: She's already won. "Come on. It's perfect. One weekend. What's the worst that could happen?" I almost believe her.

Mom and Dad are asleep when I get home, thank goodness. I need the space to think. They won't say it out loud, but dropping out of college was a failure. Still, I have this sense that there's something bigger I'm supposed to do. But every time I try, the pieces refuse to fit. Maybe this trip is what I need.

I crawl into bed and stare at the ceiling. The room feels quiet, and I try to focus on my breathing. It steadies me until exhaustion pulls me under.

Suddenly, I'm somewhere else.

The space is enormous. It looks like a cave, and it feels alive. There's a hum in the air that I feel in my bones. Light shifts, bouncing off relics that are scattered everywhere. At the center, a woman sits with her head bowed. Her skin glows and I've never seen anyone whose hair matches my own pale blond. For a moment, I wonder if it's me. When our eyes meet, fear grips me. I feel small. She sees everything I am and everything I could ever become.

***

I never quite mastered saying no to Rhu or Violet. Maybe it's because I've always been desperate for connection. The road trip isn't the grand dress rehearsal Rhu pitched. It's the same as every other trip. We light up in a parking lot, Violet's playlists loop, and Rhu fills silences.

Laughter comes easily for them. For me, it feels hollow.

The dirt road stretches out through the farmland. Acres and acres of fields dotted with tents like a sprawling village that pops up once a year for Harvest Fire. The place is owned by some local guy, and at twenty bucks a vehicle, he's making a fortune. When we get to the front of the line, a girl in an orange vest waves us toward our spot. Rhu pulls onto a patch of flattened grass next to a green VW van. Outside, our neighbors are already setting up camp. Rhu turns in her seat, grinning like a little kid.

"Hey," she says, holding up a baggie. Inside, the shrooms look shriveled and strange. "I brought these. You in?"

"I don't know..."

"Come on," Rhu says. "It's Harvest Fire. Live a little."

Violet twists around to face me. "Seriously, Skye. What's gonna happen?"

"You never know," Rhu pops a cap into her mouth and passes me the bag. "That's what makes it fun."

I shrug and comply, hoping they don't notice my unease. The moment they hit, something inside me shifts. Not just colors or sounds, but deeper. The taste of metal fills my mouth, and a flicker of green lightning cracks behind my eyes. Now, as we wander through the fields, Rhu's energy pulls me like a tether. Her dreads sway as she weaves through the crowd and Violet flits around like a firefly. As I lag behind, the ground feels unstable beneath my feet and the air presses against my skin. I tell myself it's just the shrooms, but I'm not sure. The world is shifting, stretching at the edges, like it's trying to make room for something else.

"Skye! Stop dragging your feet!" Rhu calls out.

The words feel distant and the horizon ripples at the edges. I can't tell if it's the shrooms or me. Probably both. "I'm coming," I force a smile. Someone hands me a drink and I gulp down the sweet liquid.

Rhu takes my hand, and we dance. She always knows how to entice, dangling escape in front of me like a lure. And the worst part? I always bite. The music drowns out my thoughts. Faces smear into strange masks by the firelight, and for a moment I lose myself.

Something feels off. My feet stumble, and the air is too thick to breathe. Rhu is swallowed by the crowd. I try to follow, but the bonfire seems to warp, its flames stretching up further and further toward the sky. A hand brushes my arm with fingers that are too cold and I pull away, but my body is sluggish and disconnected.

I think we're walking toward the woods. His hand is on my arm, guiding me into the dark, and I want to say something, but my mouth won't form the words. My body moves without consent, like I'm watching from behind my own eyes. Worse than the fear is the shame, like I've failed someone I don't remember being. A thought splits through the haze: She wouldn't have let this happen, but I don't know who "she" is. Just that she feels like... me.

The moon hangs above us, her light harsh against the trees. He says something again, but I can't make sense of it. I can barely keep my eyes open. The world spins while the trees sway and darkness takes over.

***

The air in the tent is stale, and I hug my knees closer. It is warm, but ice grips at my heart. I want to feel something, anything. However, the emptiness threatens to take over. I remember his eyes, colored like the sky and wine. Had I followed him into the woods? His touch lingers on my cheek, and I still hear the words that tangled together. The moon was watching, and the shadows swallowed me whole.

My body remembers more than I do. The angry scrapes down my back and the ache in my limbs. The way my skin flinches at the wind, as if even the air has turned against me. I squeeze my eyes shut and I'm back in the tent. I don't remember how we got here. My vision blurs, and I need to escape, to be anywhere but here. A flicker of movement catches my eye, and I swear I see a pixie slip outside through the tent flap. My hands fumble with the zipper, which catches as I try to pull it down.

Outside, the pale light of dawn creeps over the horizon. Rhu sits on the ground, her focus locked on rolling another joint. Violet gives me a wink, like we're sharing some unspoken secret. I force a smile, keeping my mouth shut. Part of me hopes they don't notice the way my hands tremble. If they did, I'd have to explain. Yet another part aches to be seen, to have them look past my mask and ask what's wrong. Maybe if I wish hard enough, everything will just disappear.

No one asks. So, I pull out a cigarette. I don't even like smoking, but it feels good to hold on to something. The first drag burns my lungs, grounding me. I exhale slowly, the smoke curling and disappearing into the morning. The sun will set tonight, and it will rise again tomorrow. Nothing that happened here will matter. I weave my way through the sea of tents. The warmth is a welcome caress after the moon's disdain.

The treeline is ahead, and water rushes, barraging my senses with flashes from the night before. My head jammed painfully against a rock, arms pinned, wanting to shout stop, but I just couldn't keep my eyes open.

A woman is bathing in the stream when I arrive. The sunlight is glinting off her blond hair. Breasts, dripping with water, sparkle in the light. She smiles at me, oblivious to my shame. Her eyes are deep and endless, the way dreams look just before you wake. Light moves in them, something older than memory. She feels familiar in a way that hurts. Like a mother I never knew, or a god I used to belong to.

I dip my toes into the water, losing myself in the path the stream is taking, trying to follow the tiniest of drops as it flows away. Gazing into the reflection, my face stares back. She looks so full of hope and innocence, yet I know better. I submerge myself. The rocky bed is uncomfortable, but not like the night before. Water finds its path over me, washing away the disgrace while the dappled light of the sun shines through the trees.

I am reborn.

The woman with the star-speckled eyes rises and steps into the forest, moving like she belongs to it. The trees part for her and shadows bend in her wake. I follow her and the birds do not scatter at my approach. They watch, heads tilted, as if they have been waiting. The moss is soft beneath my feet, and I slip off my sandals without thinking. I let the earth touch my skin.

I'm lost inside, but here, I feel safe. In the distance, there is music. A mournful tune that pierces deep into my soul. The mist rises, and the woman stops, stretching her hand towards me. When her fingers brush against mine, a warmth spreads through my body. She strokes my hair as I weep in her arms.

We walk together towards the music, into the mist. The smell of fresh bread permeates the air, and the tables are laden with fruit and all varieties of cakes and sweets. Beings are dancing and laughing and the musicians are scattered through the crowd, yet somehow playing as one. Some smile and acknowledge me, others move, graceful as ballerinas, lost in their own ecstasy.

The woman hands me a glass filled with honeyed nectar, and I drink it in. She touches my face in the same spot he did, but I don't recoil. She hands me a piece of warm bread. I put it to my lips. Not a word is spoken as she leads to the clearing that smells of sweet rot and growing things. Roots twist beneath the moss like veins. At the center, something pulses, half-hidden in the earth, glowing faintly like it remembers being a star. We dance and dance until my feet can no longer move and then sway slowly as the music dies out. Collapsing to the ground, sleep finally overtakes me.

When I open my eyes, the world is hollow. The woman is gone and it all vanishes like mist in the morning sun. The forest is just trees again. The wind is just wind. Something is missing. I can feel it, a part of me left behind in the clearing. Or maybe it was never mine to begin with. Two selves, still echoing inside the same skin. One who dreams of birds and firelight. The other who still trembles at the sound of her own name.

The path through the woods feels longer now. Silence is colder than the night before, clinging like fog that won't lift. Somewhere between the clearing and here, something was left behind. Two versions of me stir beneath my skin, edges raw. One recalls firelight and laughter that didn't reach her eyes. The other flinches from touch and memory. I don't know which one is real. Maybe neither is.

CHAPTER 13

The Raven

My room is large. A false freedom with just enough space to make me forget I'm still in a cage. The walls are thick, the hum of the engines distant here. The only real escape is the viewing portal, an expanse of reinforced glass on the far wall. I press my hands to the pane willing it to vanish and imagine stepping through with my arms outstretched. Instead, all I see is my own reflection, a pale shadow of the woman who calls herself my mother.

Below, a sea of poisoned clouds churns, thick and dark, spilling acid rain onto the poor souls who still cling to the surface. The people I am supposed to save. The ones waiting for a prophecy that means nothing. The livable land has thinned to ribbons, barely clinging to life. Towns that once thrived had vanished into the rifts. There were fewer lights every time we descended, like stars winking out one by one.

I shake my head and catch my reflection in the window. My face is pale, delicate, nothing like her. Where Mother is all shadows and sharp edges, I am soft. My hair is nearly white, my skin as light as the porcelain china she sips tea from. I know what they whisper. Too fragile. Too breakable.

No one knows who my father was, not even me, and The Raven doesn't tolerate the question. Those who ask too many things that don't concern them are discarded. That only needed to happen once for the lesson to stick.

After turning away, the walls close in again. Then I cross the room and pull open the wardrobe, already seeking what I need. Beneath the neat stacks of clothing, my hands find the leather straps of my wings. I don't remember the moment I decided to build them. It was instinct, as if my body had always known I was meant to fly.

They are better now, the pieces fit together and they look almost like real wings. I run my fingers over the intricate stitching, tracing the feathers one by one. Each one carefully curated, a fragment of something once free. This time, they will work.

The glider is almost finished. An intricate pattern of feathers is laced over the thin leather backing, stitched together with precision. Not true wings, but close enough. Each feather is one I found myself collected over the years. I have spent years perfecting this. A Magnum Opus of sorts. Not even Lena or Mother know I kept them.

I collapse onto my bed, flipping through my notes for what feels like the hundredth time. I run through the calculations, testing the angles in my mind. They will work. They have to.

The ship groans as we descend; the engines adjusting to the shift in altitude. I exhale. We're approaching Azuros, the largest settlement left standing on the ground.

It wasn't always like this. Before Mira liberated it, Azuros was a slave city. A labor camp disguised as civilization - a place where people were born, worked, and died under the rule of air dwellers. Mira burned their ships and left the survivors to build something new. And now, somehow, it endures. A stronghold of trade, survival, and desperation. A place where the sky-dwellers and the ground-rats pretend they can co-exist.

Somewhere down there, Lena is waiting for us.

Lena - The Owl, people call her. Sharp-eyed, sharp-tongued, and wise in a way that makes others uncomfortable. She can look straight through you and see the thing you don't want to admit, the truth you're trying to ignore.

She's also the only person in this world who loves me. Others admire me. I could step onto the deck right now, and they would kneel. Not out of love, not even out of loyalty, but because I am the child of prophecy. They do not see me. They see what I am supposed to be, a legend. My mother created this myth, and now the world swears fealty to it. But I am not the prophecy. I am just the girl who was chosen to wear it, and to my mother, I am not even that.

Lena is different. She raised me, taught me how to listen, not to Mira's sermons, but to the wind. How the world shifts if you pay attention. She goes where I cannot.

My mother keeps me safe aboard The Raven. That's how she sees it, anyway. Safer in the sky, where no one can touch me. It's better if my feet never press into real dirt, and I don't breathe the air my so-called people are choking on.

Lena walks among them. She works in the ground dweller settlements, treating the sick, ensuring them the sky hasn't forgotten them. Perhaps it's a heart for charity that moves her, but I know better. She does it because she still believes in something more than the prophecy.

Only three people know the truth - Lena, my mother, and me. And Mother doesn't even realize I know. Lena told me on my sixteenth birthday.

A knock at the door pulls me from my thoughts.

"Skye?" Derrick's voice calls. Three more quick raps follow in rapid succession. "We're about to dock. Your mother wants to see you."

"Coming." I tuck away my wings and force myself to go to the door. It isn't Derrick's fault he's been assigned to me. But that doesn't mean I want him here.

Time to face the world again.

The Raven carves through the clouds, headed to the ground. I stand beside my mother, hands folded at my sides and my face blank. As we descend, the brilliant blue fades, swallowed by thick, sulfur-stained clouds. The air turns heavy, pressing in. The airships stay above the smog, where the wind is crisp and breathing doesn't burn. Down here, survival is a different thing.

As soon as we land, gravity shifts. It's not just the pull of the earth; I feel it in my bones. My mother stands at the helm, watching me with that unreadable expression of hers. She wants me here, where they can see me. The child of prophecy. But she never lets me stray too far from the ship.

Her lips curve, the ghost of what might be a smile. "You must be pleased to see Lena again." I incline my head, saying nothing. She exhales. "Skye, you're going to have to talk to me sometime."

"I am a grown woman, Mother." The words taste wrong. "Someday, you will have to let me leave this ship." Who am I kidding? The world bows to her. Whole cities bend beneath her will. What makes me think I could ever be different? I square my shoulders. "How am I supposed to heal a world I have never touched?" The words slip out before I can stop them. They are too raw, and the air between us goes thin.

"You are so young, Skye," she says, the words almost kind. "And you did not grow up down here. You do not understand."

"Then let me," I push. "Let me go where they are."

"Tell me," she says softly. "How will you save them if you are dead?"

I scoff. "You're the one who wants to save it. Maybe you should have written the prophecy about yourself."

Her shift is subtle, but I feel it like the moment before a storm. No. No, no, no. I didn't mean to say that. I promised Lena I wouldn't. And now, I've doomed the only person who loves me. Then she exhales.

"If I could change the prophecy, I would." Her voice is too calm. "But the winds spoke to Lena, and we both know Lena would never lie."

But she did. She lied to the world. She lied about me. She didn't catch the slip. Not this time.

Then she surprises me. "We will be docked for three days. You may accompany me to the Tribunal meeting."

For a heartbeat, I let myself imagine what it would be like if she smiled because she wanted to see me happy, not because it served some purpose, but the moment passed, the way it always did.

Azuros is nothing like the smaller settlements we visit. I have never seen more than the city from the dock, but Lena once described it as a sprawling expanse teeming with all kinds of people. The Raven helped free it six or seven years ago, right around the time of my jump.

Mother is respected for her role in its revolution, but Azuros does not worship her the way smaller settlements do. The city is self-sufficient, powerful in its own right. Once it stood on its own, she needed Azuros far more than it ever needed her.

"Perhaps a trip to the market, too?" I ask, careful to keep my voice casual.

Mother lifts a brow, considering. Then, to my surprise, she relents. "Lena will be meeting us at the Tribunal. She knows the city well, and I will allow her to take you to the marketplace." Her gaze sharpens. "Derrick will accompany you, and a small guard unit will follow at a distance."

I keep my face blank, shoving down the grin threatening to slip through. Inside, my mind is already racing, piecing together possibilities, mapping out every path.

The ship completes its descent, settling into place with a low groan. A docking ramp extends, and the clamps secure The Raven with a heavy thunk. After the engines cycle down, their hum fades into silence. A small crowd gathers at the edge of the platform, voices rising in scattered cheers. Children scramble onto their parents' shoulders, pointing and whispering. Despite the poisoned clouds and crumbling cities, they still believed in something better, even if it rested on a lie. Maybe that was enough.

There she is! The Raven! She's so beautiful!

Is the child of prophecy with her?

I resist the urge to roll my eyes. I'm not a child anymore, just a pale, unimpressive woman who looks far too fragile for the legend wrapped around her. Sorry to disappoint.

Mother and I give the obligatory waves and polite smiles before retreating below deck. The moment we step away from prying eyes, her warmth vanishes. "We will disembark for the Tribunal at first light. Be ready."

Excitement crackles beneath my skin. When I reach my quarters, Derrick is already there, standing alert like a proper soldier. "When does your shift end?" I ask, letting my grin break free.

He gives me a side-eye, then smirks, throwing a light punch to my arm just like he used to when we were kids. "What's got you so excited? I don't think I've seen you smile in years."

"Mira says we can go to the market tomorrow."

The words barely leave my mouth before his body goes rigid. The playfulness drains from his face. "Azuros is dangerous, Skye..."

My head tilts. "Don't worry, you'll be with me." Then, just to get a reaction, I rise onto my toes and press a quick peck on his cheek.

It should have flustered him, but tonight, he doesn't even blink. There was a time, long ago, when Derrick would have blushed so hard he looked sunburned. When we were little, he used to follow me like a shadow, pretending to be the knight to my princess. Now, that boy is gone. The man standing before me is harder, shaped by a world that demanded too much too fast.

I sigh, stepping back. "Get some sleep. Tomorrow is going to be fun!" Derrick's jaw is set, and for a moment, I think he might say something more. Instead, he just gives a small nod and shifts his stance.

In my room, I plot my escape. My wings will have to stay since I'm on the ground now, but I reach for a couple of my favorite feathers to put on a cord around my neck. Lena will be easy to convince. She has never feared my mother, not the way others do. She loves her too much for that. But she also loves me, which means she'll give me the time I need. Mother, for all her cruelty, has always protected Lena. Derrick is the problem. He loves me in his own way, but his fear of The Raven outweighs that. My head spins as I crawl into bed, but sleep takes me the second my head hits the pillow.

Suddenly, I'm somewhere else. In the haze, I catch a flicker of something impossible, the scent of salt and the crash of ocean waves, a place I have never seen but know too well.

In this broken world, the oceans are long gone. They dried and shriveled during the fractures, when the skies split open and poisoned rain turned fertile lands to ash. All that remains are small, stubborn lakes, barely enough to sustain the people who scrape out their lives below.

Yet here, I hear an ocean. I feel its vastness, its hunger. It whispers of a world I don't know but ache for, a place where the earth and sky once met without hatred. I reach for it, desperate to remember something I have never truly seen.

The world around me flickers, a ruin caught between what it was and what it has become, and at the center, she waits, pale as bone and hair the same color as mine. For a moment, I think she is me.

Then her eyes lift, and I know this is not a reflection. She is real, she is waiting, and she knows me.

I reach for her, only to wake up.

***

The world around me is chaos. It's hard to breathe and there are too many hands reaching, grabbing for me. They want to touch my pale skin, like I'm something sacred. The guards close in, shielding me as my mother walks a step ahead. No one dares touch her. They fear her too much. She doesn't look back, but I feel her certainty. This won't do.

I force myself to stand taller, scowl sharper. A child, small and wide-eyed, reaches out. My glare lands on her and she whimpers and slinks into the shadows.

When we reach the Hall of Governance, Lena is waiting.

Before I can speak, she pulls me into a warm embrace, and just like that, I am home. The air stirs around her like even the wind bent close to hear her speak. Lena had always carried the winds with her, not just listened to them, but lived among them, the way others lived among family.

"I missed you, sweet one," she whispers as she takes my hand. If only she knew the sweetness was gone.

The Tribunal speaks. Their voices drone on and I cannot focus. My mind turns over my plan again and again. Lena is the only one I will tell. She can distract Derrick when the time comes. The meeting ends too quickly. My mother gives me a stiff hug before turning away, already deep in discussion with faction leaders. She dismisses me, just like that.

As Lena leads me toward the market, Derrick trails just a few feet behind.

"What's going on, sweet one?" Lena asks. She misses nothing when it comes to me.

That's why she told me the truth that the Prophecy never existed. It was just something made up to save me. Lena also told me Mira is not really my mother. She was the one who found me, cradled me in the wreckage of that ship, while my real mother lay lifeless beside me. They took me in, but not out of love. Out of necessity. Some twisted sense of fate she and Lena stitched together out of desperation.

Mira does not know that I know. She still believes I see her as my mother, that I wear the title daughter without question. She doesn't realize that every time she calls me her child, something fractures.

"This is my chance to leave." I say.

Lena's lips press into a sad frown. "I knew it was coming."

"I have to find out who I am," I say. "And I never will on The Raven."

Lena nods and her hands tighten around mine. She's holding back tears. "You will break her heart."

Something inside me snaps. "She doesn't have one."

Lena flinches. "Oh, child…" That's all she says. Because Mira is her weakness. No matter what she's done, Lena loves her more than she will ever love me.

I pull away. "Tell Derrick I'm sorry." Then I squeeze her hand one last time and slip into the crowd.

If I let myself think about Lena's arms pulling me close, about the lullabies she sang when I was sick, about the steady way she taught me to listen when the world grew too loud, I might never leave at all. The market is a flood of movement. I pull a hooded cloak from my pack, tucking away my pale hair. Then I weave back around, avoiding the main paths.

The moment my absence is noticed, chaos erupts. I slip through the crowd, moving toward the market gates before the exits are sealed. I don't look back. A small establishment catches my eye. Some sort of tavern, I think. I hurry inside and a man brings over a drink. The liquid inside is too thick, too sweet. I take a sip, but the flavor leaves a bad taste in my mouth. I don't finish it.

When enough time passes, I decide it's safe to leave. The streets are quieter now. I duck into an alley. I should feel exhilarated. Instead, something is wrong. The lack of sleep must be catching up with me. My vision blurs, my limbs feel heavy. My steps start to falter. My vision wavers. My limbs feel slow, heavy. I force myself forward. I am strong. I am in control. A hand closes around my wrist. Fingers press against my skin. Heat surges through me, and my body locks, instincts screaming that something is not right.

I turn and the blade is in my hand before I even register drawing it. A single movement, a whisper of steel through the air. A choked sound. A gurgle. Blood everywhere, and I see his face.

No. No, no, no. I step back. He sways, his mouth open, his eyes wide

Did I just kill Derrick?

CHAPTER 14

The Owl

Time moves strangely these days. Too fast, then too slow, then slipping through my fingers before I can catch it. The diner is the same, the shifts blending together, customers' faces already forgotten before I step outside. My hands go through the motions: pour, wipe, nod, repeat. I am there, and yet I am not.

Rhu and Violet always seem freer than me, able to shift and change direction like the wind. I feel stuck in a job that doesn't care about me, with parents who don't know me, in a world that barely sees me. I have heard little from my friends since Harvest Fire. That isn't unusual. Rhu showing up to invite me on a road trip was the anomaly, not the silence afterward. So, I let it be.

I haven't been sleeping well. My dreams have been full of strange things. Images hover just out of reach, close enough to brush against but never to grasp. I see myself in them, but not quite. The face staring back at me is terrifying, and I don't know if that should scare me or if I should want to be her. Sometimes I see a version of me that stands taller, and is fierce enough to tear down the sky itself. Sometimes it's another me altogether, hollow-eyed and dangerous, a ghost cut loose from everything she once was. I think I am just standing there, ordinary and breakable, watching them both.

According to the internet, dreaming of yourself just means you need self-reflection. Sure. Maybe. But the version of me in those dreams isn't just different. She's powerful. I can feel it just beneath the surface, like a second heartbeat. I don't have that kind of power and don't even know if I want it.

But sometimes, I think I do.

Either way, it's time to rejoin the real world, so I pick up my phone and call Vi. She answers on the second ring. "Hey, Skye, where have you been?" Her voice is confused. Like I'm the one who hasn't been around, instead of them. If she was so worried, why didn't she call first?

"Just working." I keep my tone easy. "I've missed you guys. What are you up to?"

"Oooh, Nick's having a bonfire tonight at his uncle's place in Rye! You should come!" Vi's voice is all brightness, like I was never gone at all and she didn't just vanish after Harvest Fire.

I pause. If she missed me, she never said it. If she noticed my absence, she never called. I push the thought down, keeping my voice even. "Sure. Maybe you and Rhu can catch me up on our road trip?"

A pause. Not long enough for most people to notice. But I do. "Uh, yeah. Sure, we can do that."

Nick has a lot of bonfires at his uncle's place. The guy owns a ridiculous amount of land. It used to be a farm, I think, but mostly it's just an excuse for parties. Not so different from

Harvest Fire. The thought of having a drink makes my stomach twist. At least these are people I know. People I went to high school with. That should make it feel safer. It doesn't.

"I'll See you tonight." Then I hang up before she can say anything else. My stomach drops. That pause could mean nothing. But I know it doesn't. I knew, deep down, that our trip was a whim. That I was the only one hanging onto it like a lifeline. Maybe I'm wrong. But I don't think I am. Tonight, I'll go to the party. I'll listen to what they have to say. But if they've already let go of the plan, then I'll tell them my truth.

I'm going anyway.

***

I drive alone to the party, showing up later than I'd intended. Above me, the stars are poking through the early September sky. Summer is still fighting to hold on, but autumn is on its way. The quiet solitude of the drive gave me a strange sense of finality, like I was heading toward a last hurrah before everything changed.

As soon as I park, I can see the bonfire in the center of a loose ring of people, tongues of orange licking the night air. There's a keg on one side and a series of coolers full of beer on the other. A local band is playing somewhere off to the right. People stand around in clusters, leaning close to hear each other's voices over the music. The entire scene glows and the smell of smoke and burning wood mixes with spilled beer.

The second I step closer, the old excitement I used to feel at parties like this flares up inside me. Once upon a time, this was all I wanted: beautiful music, laughter, and reckless freedom. Tonight, there's a knot in my stomach. I'm not sure if it's nerves or a sadness about leaving Portsmouth.

I spot Rhu first. She's with a group of people I know only in passing. For a moment, I wonder if she's realized I've been "missing in action," as Violet would say. Vi is standing in the shadowy space near a cooler, scanning the crowd like she's searching for something more interesting than what she's got. I make a beeline for her.

"Hey, Vi." I raise my voice so she can hear me over the music.

She turns, a bright smile stretching across her face. She greets me with a hug that's warm in action but stiff in emotion. I feel how quickly she withdraws. It's like there's an invisible wall between us. "Hey, you! I'm glad you made it," she says.

I hug my arms around myself. "Crazy night," I offer, trying to sound casual. "So... what's up with the road trip?"

The words come out before I can stop them. Pull the Band-Aid off, I tell myself. If they're going to bail, I want to know now, and I want to hear her say it.

Violet's eyes flick away from mine. "Oh... yeah." She scratches at her forearm, looking sheepish. "We've been meaning to tell you. You kinda went missing for a bit, and, well... we put it off until next summer."

There it is. No preamble, no apology, just the truth dumped in my lap. "Next summer," I repeat, doing my best to keep my voice steady.

"Yeah, the guys want to follow the band on tour for a while, and we figured we could all go together." She shrugs, smiling like it's no big deal. "You could come along with us." Something in my chest tightens, and I'm watching a door close in front of me. The trip wasn't a promise, not to them. It was just another idea, something fleeting in the same way most things are to people like Rhu and Violet.

"I... I'm still thinking of going by myself."

Her eyebrows jump in surprise. "By yourself?" Then she laughs. "You don't even have a car, Skye. Is your mom going to let you have hers?"

I force a small smile. That's never stopped me from dreaming. A part of me had hoped she would say something else - like, 'Don't go, Skye, we need you.' Or at least, 'We'll make it work, we'll leave tonight if that's what you want.' Instead, she laughs. I swallow hard. "You're right." My voice sounds robotic, even to me. "Gonna go mingle."

I can't stand to linger with her, so I wander away, weaving through groups of people who've formed tight huddles around each other. Beer sloshes in red cups; smoke and laughter drift in the night air. Someone thrusts a half-empty bottle of something in my direction, but I shake my head. I spot Chris, who I partied with a lot back in the day. For a moment, I think talking to him might ground me, might offer some comfort.

"Hey, Chris." I ease into the small circle he's part of. Their conversation fades for a second as he turns to me with a vague look of recognition.

"Oh, hey - Skye, right? Weren't you at Plymouth State or something?"

"Yeah," I reply. "I left after a semester. College just... wasn't for me."

He nods like he's heard it a million times. "Right on. So what're you up to now?"

My cheeks heat. I can't tell if he's interested or just making conversation. "I'm leaving tomorrow." I search his expression for the slightest sign of surprise. "For a trip."

"Nice." It's the kind of polite response you give at a party. "When you coming back?" Ouch. The casual question hits me right in the chest, because it assumes I'm just another drifter who can't commit to anything. And it also shows he doesn't know me. Never did.

"I don't think I am."

"Cool," he replies, and then his attention is back on his group. Someone's talking about a concert coming up in a few weeks, and Chris turns away, reabsorbed in their conversation. I stand there for another second, feeling hollow.

Eventually, I back away. My gaze drifts across the bonfire. In the wavering glow, I see Rhu, Violet, and a bunch of others, laughing like no one has a care in the world. An ache floods my chest again. At one point, these people felt like family. Our whole lives were about stepping into the unknown together. Now it's as if I'm wearing an invisibility cloak; I can fade into the background, slip through conversations, and no one stops me.

I realize then that no one is going to ask me to stay. In truth, I'm not even sure I want them to. But there's a naïve part of me that wishes someone would try - that maybe one of them would see me drifting away and be afraid to lose me. The music dies down between sets. Someone is fiddling with a guitar amp, and the lull is awkward enough that everyone's eyes wander.

"I'm heading out," I say, wondering if it will change anything. A few heads turn. Rhu waves lazily. Violet gives me a thumbs-up without looking away from whoever's talking.

Then conversation flows over the moment smoothing it away like a tide erasing footprints in the sand, and everything just moves on. I guess deep down; I knew this would happen. There's no anger, no shock. Just an empty acceptance that things have changed, and maybe they've been changing for a long time.

I turn away from the fire. The flames still roar behind me, and bursts of laughter erupt here and there, and the band starts back up. No one stops me. No one calls my name. When I look back one final time, it is as if I had never existed. The grass is damp with evening dew, and the smell of smoke lingers on my clothes as I head back to my car. I'm aware of how quiet the world is once I step away from the circle of light and noise. My eyes sting with tears that I refuse to shed.

The music is faint now, replaced by the steady hum of the engine. I breathe in, then out, finding a strange relief in knowing that I'm finally letting go of something that was never mine to begin with. My parents are still awake when I get home. The news drones on in the background. Mom has her laptop open, eyes scanning something I'll never ask about. Who even watches the news anymore?

"Hey, kiddo," Dad calls out.

I pause at the doorway to the den. I owe a goodbye. They're the only parents I've ever known. Distant, sure, but they love me in their own way. Mom senses something. Her focus lifts from the laptop, but she says nothing.

"I'm leaving in the morning."

Dad cocks his head, and Mom narrows her eyes. "I take it you don't mean for work," she says. "I figured something was up with that ugly van your friend brought around."

I consider lying, saying I'm not going alone. But I am. And they'll figure it out. "Yeah. That trip didn't work out," I admit. "I'm going on my own."

Dad nods, like somewhere inside, he understands. Mom shuts her laptop. Mom's fingers hover over her laptop keyboard, her face unreadable. "What's your plan?" she asks, like she's asking about a business deal, not my life.

"I don't have one," I admit.

She exhales, slowly. Then, to my surprise, she closes the laptop. "At least map out where you're going before you leave." It's more concern than I expected.

"This is something she needs, Maggie," Dad says. His voice is calm, but his eyes are full of something he's not saying. He stands and pulls me into a hug. "Call us if you're in trouble, all right?"

The lump in my throat is sudden and I nod against his shoulder. My heart aches in a way I didn't expect.

***

I lied when they dropped me off at the Greyhound station. I'm taking a bus west, I had told them. Instead, I grabbed some breakfast. The Friendly Toast is just a couple of blocks from the bus stop. It seemed a better bet than going to the Sunshine Diner, as I had just quit with no notice.

I eat my toast and eggs and stare out the window, watching the seagulls wheel overhead. The sky is dark and the gulls seem to sense a storm. They let out their shrill cries, and a gust of wind pushes against the diner's windows, rattling them in their frames. The air doesn't smell like rain should. It carries a metallic tang that stings the back of my throat. It reminds me of the dreams I have where the air is wrong and clouds choke out the stars. Maybe this is where the world is headed and the future is bleeding into me.

I should head out before it pours. I'm not sure why I decided hitchhiking was a good idea. Clean slate, maybe. I guess I am embracing my invisibility. After paying my bill, I step outside. The wind has picked up, and the first fat drops of rain splatter against the pavement. I pull my hoodie tighter and start walking toward I-95.

Once I get close enough to the freeway, I stick my thumb out. The cars blur past, their headlights gleaming off the wet road. Most people don't even slow down. Most people would say it's stupid to hope for kindness in a world like this, but here I am, drenched, shaking, and still holding my hand out to the storm. Maybe that's what surviving really is; trusting that somewhere, somehow, someone might still stop.

After what feels like hours, I'm soaked to the bone and my clothes are clinging to my skin. I'm rethinking my no-buses decision. There's no shame in a bus ticket. At least to Boston.

Just as I'm about to turn back, headlights cut through the rain. A Jeep Cherokee slows to a stop, tires kicking up a spray of water. The wind howls through the underpass, rattling the road signs. My hoodie is soaked through, the rain sliding down my arms, clinging to my skin.

The man leans out, all white teeth and easy charm. "Where are you headed in this mess?"

"Anywhere."

His passenger leans over, a woman. They are both young, maybe mid-twenties, but something about her makes my stomach twist. Maybe it's the way she studies me. "You're not a runaway, are you?" Her accent lilts, something not quite Irish.

I shake my head, trying to swallow the apprehension. "No."

The man grins. The woman doesn't. Her gaze flicks to the sky, then back to me. "Then hop in."

CHAPTER 15

THE RAVEN

My eyes struggle to adjust to the hazy light as I blink them open. A slow, pounding ache throbs behind my temples. The air is stale and burns the back of my throat. I inhale, forcing the nausea down. The industrial rot is familiar. It permeates everything in ground dweller settlements, and my lungs aren't used to breathing it.

A rough blanket is draped over me, the fibers coarse against my skin. I shove it aside, but the scent lingers: damp wood, sweat, something metallic. I shift, and the mattress beneath me feels lumpy and uneven. It's not the plush cushion of my bed on The Raven. I inhale and my throat burns as stale air scrapes against raw nerves. The ground is an unforgiving place.

Then events come back in flashes. Fear. Confusion. Blood. I am not used to fear. It is an abstract thing, something that happens to other people, something I watch from above. The tavern. That thick drink. The blurred edges of movement. Did someone drug me? The wet warmth of blood on my hands.

I bolt upright. My eyes rake across the room, pulling in details as fast as I can. It is small, but clean. Not the kind of filth I expected down here, though "clean" is relative in this place. The walls are bare, the air dry. No smell of sickness. My fingers reach my hip, but my dagger isn't there.

I scan the floor to find my pack is in the corner with my cloak and clothing folded beside it. My dagger rests on top. Clean. If I had stabbed someone, there would be blood, wouldn't there?.

The blanket has no signs of lice or bed bugs. Still, my skin crawls. I hate being vulnerable like this. After pushing back the unease, I shift to my feet and crouch beside my pack and unbuckle the straps. Everything is still here. Nothing taken, but no clues, either. The light filtering through the uneven slats of the window tells me it's midmorning - I think. But I don't trust my sense of time in this haze. The sky down here is a liar.

When I fasten my cloak, I make sure the hood covers my hair and shadows my face. Then I breathe, rolling my shoulders, testing my limbs. The initial rush of panic has faded, and it's time to figure out what happens next. From what I see, I have two viable options. Try to leave; find the nearest gate and disappear into the world before my mother's reach catches up to me, or find my way back; swallow my pride and return to The Raven.

I flex my fingers, rolling my shoulders and testing for injuries. My mother's voice is in my head. "You let yourself get caught. You let yourself be vulnerable. And now look at you - weak and lost." My jaw locks. She's right. I was careless and missed the angles, failed to plan ahead. A mistake like that doesn't go unpunished. She taught me better than this. And yet, here I am.

The answer should be simple: return, regroup, fix this before my mother finds me. That's what she would demand, but the thought of setting foot on The Raven again makes my stomach turn. Derrick would have found me by now. If I had waited, he would have come. Loyal to a fault, always watching my back even when I pushed him away. I wonder if he's searching for me now, if he even had a choice.

I close my eyes, pressing my nails into my palms. My mother's voice whispers at the edge of my thoughts. *You are the future. You are too important to waste yourself on carelessness.* And yet the wind outside shifts, and for a fleeting second, something else is calling to me. I don't know what it is, but I know I don't want to go back.

Outside, the streets are empty except for an ancient woman on a rocker in front of a door that looks identical to mine. All the doors on this street have the same peeling paint and a sense of quiet despair. I look her way and she's staring at me the way a deckhand on The Raven would watch the cogs to decide if the debris is a threat to the engines. Apparently, I'm not worth worrying about. She gives a sniff and goes back to staring at nothing. Then I step closer and clear my throat.

"Where is everyone?" I ask, trying to sound casual. It still comes out sounding just a little like an order.

"Eh?" Her voice comes out like gravel. Then she barks out a laugh. "Most are at the rally." She gestures westward with a gnarled hand. Now that I'm listening, I can hear the low murmur of a crowd gathering somewhere in the distance.

"Do you always sit out here?" Maybe she saw something.

She grunts.

"Did you see who brought me here?" I press, feeling the edge of my voice go tight.

She lets out a ragged laugh. "New to the business? Always make 'em pay first, dearie."

I blink, my mouth half-open. "What?"

She gives me a once-over, like I'm both naive and not worth educating. Her eyes flick to my hips, back to my face, and then she shakes her head. It lands on me a moment later: She thinks I'm a prostitute. My cheeks flare hot, and I open my mouth to tell her exactly how wrong she is, but she's already closed her eyes and is rocking again, leaving me standing there like some half-witted fool. Then her snores begin rattling through the air and cut off any chance of correcting her.

I turn toward the rising voices, their energy echoing through the narrow streets. The closer I get, the more the alleys fill with people packed tighter than the markets. Their hollow-eyed stares are fixed on the square, and no one spares me a second glance.

At the center of it all, a makeshift podium has been thrown together from salvaged wood and old shipping crates. A man stands atop it, his gaze sweeping over the crowd. His voice rises and crashes, raw with fury. The crowd surges beneath him, their restless energy turning feverish. Something about the set of his shoulders tugs at a memory. His hair and beard have gone gray, but there's nothing frail about him. I squint, the years peeling away in my mind, and suddenly, I know him.

Elder Kashan. A face I have not seen since I was a child. His village was the one place Mother would ever let me disembark, and I had loved every minute of my time on the ground. Kashan wasn't like the others. He never bowed, never treated me like a symbol or a promise. I remember him lifting me onto his shoulders, and saying. "Hold tight, little bird."

His voice made me feel safe. Nothing like the angry, fire-stoked voice that lashes through the crowd now. Watching him now, I feel like I'm seeing a ghost. I used to trust him. He was the first person who spoke to me like I was real, not a prophecy wrapped in skin. He carried me on his shoulders, told me the stars belonged to no one. That I could take them for myself. Now, his voice is steel that lashes at the crowd.

"The Raven is no savior! She is no different from the air-dwellers she claims to oppose! She steals, she hoards, she dangles hope like a prize you will never be allowed to claim!" His words don't just turn against my mother. They turn against me and everything I was raised to believe. The worst part is he's right.

I slip into the shadows, pressing my back against a crumbling wall. As I wait for him to say more, I look at the surrounding people. Their dark hair hangs in brittle clumps, some of them balding in uneven patches. Skin, pockmarked and weathered by sun, stretches too tight over sharp bones.

I glance down at my own smooth, unmarked body, pale as polished bone. This should have been me. Would have been, if Lena and Mira hadn't stolen me from whatever fate the ground had planned. A tear pricks at the corner of my eye before I can stop it. Then I hear my mother's voice in my mind. *You are their savior. Save your tears for the pillow.* I can feel her nails digging into the skin just below my knuckles in reprimand. I blink hard and the tears disappear.

"Reclaim the Earth." People shout "The Sky Pirates are No Better than Air Dwellers!"

Is that what they call my mother? A sky pirate?

The masses roar their approval as Kashan raises a fist. I don't need to hear him speak to know he has them in the palm of his hand. I've seen this before. My mother does the same thing. "The Raven is no savior!" he calls out. "She is no different from the air-dwellers she claims to oppose! She steals, she hoards, she dangles hope like a prize. One you will never be allowed to claim!" The crowd erupts, shouts of anger rising like a wave.

"The prophecy is a lie!" he presses on. "A story spun to keep you waiting, to keep you obedient while she tightens her grip! Salvation will not descend from the skies, it will rise from the ground, from you! I was there. I heard the whispers of salvation, the promise that The Raven's child would lift us from the dust." A murmur rolls through the crowd, low and uneasy, and I dig my fingernails into my palms. I am that child. I don't know what unsettles me more, the accusations against my mother, or the knowledge that he is right.

"Tell me," Kashan continues, "has the prophecy fed you? Has it given you medicine? Has it kept your children safe?" Some people look away. "You wait." Kashan's voice rises. "You wait for the skies to part, for salvation to descend upon you like some divine storm. But tell me, how many of your own have you buried while waiting?" The air shifts. A woman makes a quiet, broken sound.

A man clenches his fists at his sides. "No more." The crowd erupts.

"Reclaim the Earth!" someone shouts.

"The Sky Pirates are No Better than the Air Dwellers!"

I flinch. Sky Pirates. That's what they call my mother. Then Mira steps forward. The noise doesn't stop, but it changes. There's a hesitation now, a wariness that wasn't there before. She doesn't look at Kashan. She looks at them.

"My daughter is missing."

I shouldn't be surprised. Of course, she would come here and make it a performance. I hate her for using me. I ache for her to find me. And Lena, who taught me how to listen for the truth beneath the lies, stands at her side and says nothing.

"She is young and alone in a world that will tear her apart if I do not find her first." Her voice is softer than I expected. Measured. She knows exactly what she's doing. I hate how well I recognize it. My Mother scans the crowd. She doesn't know I'm here. But she's looking for me.

"Please."

Then Lena steps forward. She doesn't stand next to Mira, just close enough to be counted as with her. She hasn't told Mira. She hasn't betrayed me.

"My daughter is not meant for this place," My mother's voice is velvet and steel. "She belongs with me. Bring her home," she pauses, then delivers the final blow. "And you will be rewarded beyond your imagination."

Excitement ripples through the crowd. The meaning is clear. Mira doesn't need an army. She just turned every desperate soul in Azuros into her hunters. My mother just put a price on me.

I have to go now. The press of bodies tightens, closing in from all sides, and the air turns thick with sweat, smoke, and decay. I slip between gaps and duck beneath outstretched arms. The square is a trap waiting to snap shut, but the alleys still offer a way out.

As I weave through the streets of Azuros, the city shrinks behind me. I keep to the routes where no one looks very hard - the places people pretend don't exist. I'm used to eyes tracking my every move, but here, no one cares who I am. Here, I am not a prophecy, not the daughter of The Raven. I am nothing. It's liberating.

The city's edge is where civilization stops pretending. Roads crumble into dirt and are swallowed by filth and neglect. Old shacks lean together, their walls patched with scrap metal and desperation. The land is sick, the decay spreading faster than the cities can retreat. Water dries up, the soil cracks, and each rift storm steals a little more of what remains.

This is where the forgotten go - the ones The Raven left behind.

A child, ribs pressing sharp against bruised skin, picks through a pile of garbage. A little further, a woman huddles beneath the broken arch of a doorway, her body curled around something too small to see. How do you save something that's already lost? Maybe the world is broken beyond saving. Maybe I'm broken too, but somewhere deep, I don't believe that. If even one thing still breathes, it isn't too late. I swallow and push forward, trying to outrun my thoughts. The air shifts and kicks up loose sand and twisting it into thin tendrils. Azuros' jagged skyline is already vanishing behind me.

Beyond the city walls, the wasteland stretches out, already half-consumed by the rising winds. Each gust stings against exposed skin, grains of sand needling into the cracks of my cloak.

The wind moves wrong. It isn't just the howling or the sting of sand. It pulls like it wants something from me. Something older inside me I had almost forgotten. A thread stretched across worlds. I don't know how I know it, but I have felt this before. The sky darkens too fast, swallowing the city behind me. Lena once told me the winds are as old as the stars. If you listen hard enough, they will carry messages. I wish I had listened better and asked her how to know when the winds want you to follow them, and when they want you to run.

I force my legs to move, but the storm is alive. The ground shifts beneath me and I stumble. Sand rises, curling around my feet. The ruins are ahead. So close. I reach for them. Then the wind slams into me.

A shadow looms in the distance, half-buried ruins jutting from the sand. The remnants of the long-dead structure swallowed by time. I don't know what it used to be, perhaps a way station or an outpost. Right now, it's the only thing standing between me and the storm.

I break into a run, head down, lungs burning. The world shrinks to nothing but the pounding of my feet and the looming shadow of the ruins ahead. Just a little farther. A gust slams into me, stealing the breath from my lungs. I choke, gasping, but the air is thick with grit, scraping against my throat like ground glass. The wind shifts without warning, pounding into my side, and suddenly, I'm off balance. My knees hit the sand first. I try to push up, but the storm is pressing me down, filling my mouth, my nose, my lungs. Every breath is a battle against suffocation. The world narrows to nothing but exhaustion.

Then hands are dragging me up. A solid warmth presses against my side and an arm locks around my waist. My body sags, too weak to fight, too tired to care. I feel myself being lowered onto rough stone. The storm rages, but I am already fading. The world turns soft at the edges. No. No, stay awake, but I can't. The storm pulls at me even now, clawing at something unseen. Like it knows me. Then, nothing.

CHAPTER 16

The Jeep pulls onto I-95 North, and an awkward silence settles over us. I've never hitchhiked before, and yet, the silence feels familiar. The kind of pause that settles when you step into someone else's life for a moment before slipping away again.

I don't know where I want to go. I don't know if I've ever known. There's not much north of here unless we're heading to Canada, and I didn't think to bring my passport. I should say something. I open my mouth to speak just as the driver clears his throat.

He chuckles. "I've never picked up a hitchhiker before," he admits, flashing a lopsided grin. "We're heading toward Acadia. Does anywhere along the way work for you?"

Acadia National Park. I haven't been there since before high school, back when our little family was still new, still learning how to exist together. Dad had taken us camping in the park, but Mom hated it, so we bailed after one night and checked into a resort instead. I remember the cliffs and the smell of pine, the way the ocean crashed against the rocky shoreline, relentless and wild. It was beautiful. Maine is as good a place as any to start.

"If you don't mind," I say, my voice coming out softer than I intend, "I think I'd like to go there. You can drop me off as close to a campground as possible." I glance at my pack. At least I came prepared.

The woman smiles. "I'm Muirenn, by the way, and this guy is my brother, Micah." Her accent hooks me, and I feel like I could listen to her talk forever.

Micah chuckles. His accent is mild New England. "So, first time hitchhiking?" He shoots me a quick glance, like he already knows the answer. I shrug. "Yeah, figured. You've got that 'not sure if this was a terrible idea' look." He taps the steering wheel, his smile turning mischievous. "But hey, first-time hitchhiker, first-time hitchhiker picker-upper - guess we're both winging it." I let out a laugh, some of my tension slipping away.

Micah gestures between himself and Muirenn. "We weren't raised together, if that's what you're trying to figure out." That explains the difference in accents. The oddest part isn't that I'm in a car with two strangers. It's that I don't feel like one. Conversation flows effortlessly, as if we've done this before and I've known them longer than the space between us should allow. I'm not great with new people, but with them, it doesn't feel like work. The words spill out before I can stop them. And for once, someone listens.

I tell them about dropping out of college, about the road trip that never happened, about Rhu and Vi ditching me at the last second. I don't mean to, but it all slips out, and somehow, I don't feel weird about it. They reciprocate. Turns out, they're twins. Muirenn was raised by their mother, while Micah grew up with their father.

"I spent half my childhood in Seattle, the other half in Bar Harbor," Micah says. "After high school, I went to MIT, got my PhD in physics." He shrugs like he didn't just drop the biggest flex in existence.

"You're a physicist?" I blink. "You seem way too... chill for that."

Micah laughs. "Yeah, I get that a lot." Muirenn gives Micah a look, but when I ask where she grew up, she hesitates.

"Everywhere, really." She says it like it should be enough, like the words are a locked door she isn't ready to open. I don't push. But something inside me knows that whatever she isn't saying matters.

The drive slips past in a dreamlike blur. One minute, I'm watching the landscape shift from civilization to wildness, the next, we're crossing into Acadia. The smell of pine permeates the air, and salt and earth blends with it in a way that feels magical.

A pressure builds in my ribs that is unfamiliar. Not fear or discomfort. Recognition.

I don't know why, but sitting here, under these stars, I matter in a way I never have before. They see me. Not as an afterthought or a name they might forget tomorrow. They decided I was worth knowing. Now, it's ending. Soon, we'll say our goodbyes. They'll drive away, and I will step into whatever this walkabout is supposed to be.

"Would you just drop me at the first campground with a vacancy?" I ask. I have my pack, and my gear. If all the campgrounds are full, I'll figure something out. Wilderness camping isn't allowed in the park, but if I don't light a fire and keep my head down, no one should bother me.

Micah and Muirenn go quiet. It's almost like they're having a conversation I'm not privy to. Maybe a twin thing? "There's an old sea cave that's pretty incredible," Micah says after a moment. "Have you been there?"

My skin warms with embarrassment. We stayed in the resort when I was here last. My mom's version of "roughing it" involves nothing more strenuous than eating trail mix in the car while admiring the scenery through a window. I shake my head. "No."

Micah glances at my pack. "Looks like you're prepared to do some off-the-beaten-path camping. Want to join us?"

"You can only get to the cave at low tide, so we will go there mid-morning tomorrow." Muirenn adds.

"I'd love it," I say. "But I thought you were headed back to Bar Harbor?"

The siblings share another glance. A tiny voice in my head reminds me that this is how people get murdered in true crime podcasts. And yet, I want to be around them.

"Muirenn isn't super comfortable around my family here," Micah finally answers. There's a story there, but I don't ask. Like everything else with them, the answer will come when it's meant to.

We hike a couple miles and make camp. By evening, a small fire crackles, its warmth pulling me in. Beyond it, I can hear the gentle waves of the Atlantic lapping at the shore. The sound washes over me. For the first time in a while, I feel still. It is as if I am part of the universe rather than an afterthought. Maybe the world is stitched together by tiny moments like this. A fire against the dark or a voice calling you back when you fall too far. Maybe that's enough to keep going.

Above, tiny pricks of light emerge, tentative at first, then bolder as the last traces of sunset fade. The reds and oranges have slipped beneath the horizon, leaving behind a sky that is a deep blue. It reminds me of Muirenn and Micah's eyes. I can't quite decide if they belong to the sea, flecked with foam and shifting with the tide, or if they are more like the night, scattered with stars. Maybe they are both. Maybe the ocean is just the sky's reflection, and we are all part of the same infinity, no matter where we stand.

Muirenn studies me, as if I am something she's trying to piece together. I pretend not to notice. We talk about our childhoods more. When I share my memory loss, they don't react the way most people do. There is no pity, just quiet acceptance. Still, I catch the way Muirenn's eyes narrow.

Micah is the more charismatic of the two, words spilling as he talks about his childhood in Seattle. The move to Maine had been hard, uprooting to a place where everything moved slower. He only adjusted when he discovered he had another sister. Apparently, he has a younger one too, though he does not linger on that part of the story.

Muirenn speaks less, but when she does, her words are careful. She tells me a little about her mother, and from what I gather, she sounds a lot like mine. Distant, focused on her work, treating relationships as something secondary. I wonder if Muirenn's teenage years were as lonely as mine. If she ever sat in a room full of people and still felt unseen.

Eventually, my thoughts slip toward sleep. I excuse myself and set up my hammock between two sturdy pines. The sky is clear, stretching wide above me with no hint of rain. I watch the trees sway against the night, their shapes dark against the deep blue. As tired as I am, sleep does not come easily. I slow my breath, trying to meditate myself into rest. Micah and Muirenn do not speak for a long time, and just as my breathing evens out, Muirenn's voice drifts across the stillness.

"She looks like one of the First Ones." Silence. The kind that is full of something unsaid.

Then Micah's voice lowers. "You'll have to help me out. I'm not as versed in Isdralan's history as you are." Isdralan. The word slips into my bones like it belongs there. It means nothing to me, but it is everything.

Muirenn answers. "Before the Guardians, there were explorers - "

A sharp sting interrupts her words. A mosquito has landed on my arm, its tiny body bloating as it feeds. I flick it away, and the moment shatters. The voices go silent. I hold still, breath steady, waiting for them to continue. But they do not. The night settles back into quiet, but my mind stirs. Isdralan. I have never heard that name before. Who are the First Ones? Why would I look like them? Muirenn spoke like she knew. Is she a historian? Or is this something else, something older?

The questions tangle in my mind, slipping between the stars like threads unraveling from the fabric of the night. I close my eyes and try to push them away. My hammock sways beneath me. Then the world shifts, and a breeze brushes my face. I open my eyes, and the trees are gone. The world is a vast and gaping maw, with the stars stretching too far apart. The ground is no longer beneath me. I am falling.

The air tears past me. I reach. Nothing. A scream, mine - but not mine, rips from my throat. Above me, the ship looms. She watches. She reaches, and I fall. The sky splits open, and I plummet, my body unraveling, bones dissolving into ribbons of light and shadow. I tear apart, and I do not know if I am being destroyed or remade. She isn't a stranger, but the piece of me built from storm and hunger, the version that survived when everything else broke. She waits for me beyond the horizon and somehow, I am falling toward her.

Then water crashes over me, rushing into my mouth and lungs. The sea drags me down, and the world above distorts. I do not fight it, but a voice calls to me.

"Wake up." The words ripple through the water, bending the darkness. "Wake up, Skye!"

Something ancient stirs. Then hands grip my shoulders, tearing me from the depths. I gasp, my lungs filling with air instead of water. My body jerks upright, trembling and drenched in sweat. The scent of fire and earth replaces salt and sea.

Micah doesn't rush to fill the silence. Muirenn's hands stay steady on my shoulders, anchoring me like she's done this before. "Skye," she says, her voice a tether pulling me the rest of the way back. "You were having a night terror. We couldn't wake you." Micah stands behind her, worry flickering across his face.

Something is missing. I feel hollow, like I woke up without all my pieces, and not just the ones I know. There's another me out there, sharper, wilder, and she's slipping further away.

I press my palms to my face, inhaling sweat and smoke and grounding myself in the present, but the dream clings to me. These nightmares have not taken me since the Hartwells took me in, so why does it feel like I never woke up?

CHAPTER 17

THE RAVEN

My face is raw, my skin burning with each breath, and at first, I think I've gone blind. My eyes refuse to open, sealed with grit. My fingers twitch as they drag against rough stone, and the pain sends a sharp bolt through my body.

This isn't how it's supposed to be. I am the child of prophecy, the heir to The Raven, and the girl destined to save this world. I was never supposed to end up here, half-buried and broken. Why do I hurt so much?

I force my fingers to move, feeling out my surroundings without revealing that I'm awake. When I pry my eyes open, the world is hazy with dust. The stone walls blend into the sand beneath me, an endless stretch of suffocating brown. Above, the roof is dilapidated, barely holding back the ugly green-gray sky the ground dwellers are forced to live under. I shift just enough to take in the rest of the space. In the corner, a figure sits cross-legged. A man, I think. He jerks his head up.

"Welcome back to the world of the living."

The voice jolts through me, familiar and unwanted, and a million feelings crash into me at once. Anger, relief, fear, hurt: they tangle, and I shove them all down. He stands, moving closer. That's when I see the bandage wrapped around his waist. So it was him I stabbed. The realization should bring clarity, but all I feel is exhaustion.

I swallow hard, forcing my voice to stay steady. "What are you doing here?"

He smirks like this is some kind of joke. "You're welcome," Derrick says.

"You should've just left me."

"I could have," he agrees. "But I didn't."

My relationship with Derrick has been strained ever since the jump all those years ago. As a kid, he was my best friend and brother in every way that mattered. He rocked me to sleep when I was scared, kept me company when loneliness crept in. We played, we laughed, and for a time, the world felt simple.

I never found out how my mother reacted after I fell. I drifted in and out of consciousness, and Derrick was gone. I remember asking Lena for my brother, but her lips stayed sealed. When he returned, something had shifted. The laughter between us had faded, replaced by distance I didn't understand. I couldn't confide in him anymore. It was as if my mother had convinced him that I wasn't a sibling to love; I was a prophecy to serve.

"Why did you follow me?" My voice is accusing. "You had your chance to run back to your precious Mira."

Derrick's eyes widen at the casual drop of my mother's name. "You didn't want me around," Derrick says without anger or accusations. That makes it worse. If he was angry, I could fight him. If he blamed me, I could push back. Instead, he just stands there, bleeding and looking at me like I'm still worth saving.

I scoff, masking the way my throat tightens. "Liar. You're nothing but Mira's pet. Too afraid to make her angry."

Derrick flinches but doesn't argue. "You're right. I am afraid of her. But I love you more than I fear her." Those words hit hard and I don't know what to do with them. Derrick doesn't let the silence stretch. "And it wasn't always like this." Outside, the wind has died, leaving only the bleak emptiness of the land stretching ahead. Derrick stands, wincing as he adjusts his bandage, then extends a hand. "Storm's clear for now. You can leave if you want."

I stare at him. "You're not going to stop me?"

He shrugs. "No. But I won't let you walk into the wasteland blind."

"So you're just going to follow me, anyway?"

His expression doesn't change. "Do you even know where you're going?"

Heat flares in my face. "Of course I do," I snap.

Derrick sees right through it. He doesn't have to say anything. I hate how easily he reads me. I don't even know where I'm going. I don't even know who I am without The Raven. The thought slams into me like a fist to the ribs. I was raised for one thing, shaped by hands that carved me into a prophecy. A weapon with a future I never asked for. The realization breaks something in me. The tears come fast, hot, ugly, and suddenly, Derrick is there. He kneels beside me, arms wrapping around me, holding me like I'm that little girl who used to crawl into his bunk when the storms rattled the ship.

"The prophecy is a lie," I choke out between shuddering sobs. "I need to understand my purpose. I need to know why I exist."

Derrick doesn't argue. He doesn't tell me what to do or try to fix it, just holds me. Then he cups my face in his hands.

"We need to go back."

I jerk away, anger surging. What was I thinking, trusting him? "No!" My breath catches in my throat. "I won't go back to The Raven - "

Derrick shakes his head, that sad, knowing smile. "Not to the ship. Back to where it all started. The crash near my village."

I blink. "You have a village?"

"Had." Derrick corrects. "It was destroyed years ago. But we were both born there. It's where Lena created her prophecy. Maybe there's evidence or proof of why she made it up."

I blink, thrown off. "You believe me that the prophecy is fake?"

Derrick doesn't hesitate. "Of course. Why wouldn't I?" I never gave much thought to the fact that Derrick wasn't born on The Raven. A pang of guilt twists in my gut. I never even thought to ask. "It's a day's walk. Let's get as close as we can tonight." He's more prepared than I am. He hands me a ration bar, then my pack, heavier than before. For once, I'm speechless. I chew the bar and follow.

The land stretches endlessly, a ruin of what once was. Bones of cities long abandoned, skeletons of roads leading nowhere. The wind kicks up dust, sifting it through the cracked remains of buildings and broken signs that no longer bear names.

I hate it down here. Everything feels too still, too close. The sky is wrong. It doesn't move the way it does above the clouds.

Up there, the air sings, the ship hums with life. There are always currents, shifting, and engines thrumming beneath my feet. Here, the ground is dead. I tighten the straps of my pack and glance at Derrick. He moves easily, his steps sure and eyes scanning the horizon for threats. I wonder if this place feels like home to him.

"What was it like?" The question escapes before I can stop it. "Growing up down here?"

Derrick laughs but doesn't look at me right away. "I don't remember too much. I was pretty young when I joined the crew of The Raven."

I wait for him to continue. He doesn't.

I frown. "That's it?"

A flicker of amusement crosses his face. "What do you want me to say?"

I didn't know. I've spent my whole life hearing stories about the wasteland. They made it sound like nothing survived down here - like the ground was only full of ghosts - but Derrick survived, and so did his village.

"You had people, though."

He nods. "Yeah." Then he adds, "I don't remember my parents. They died when I was too young to understand. It was Elder Kashan and his wife who raised me. They took in kids who had no one else." I hadn't expected him to answer so plainly.

"I know that name. He is the one who spoke the other day. At that rally." Derrick glances at me then, surprise flitting across his features before he nods. I never imagined Derrick with parents, much less a whole life before The Raven. I had never thought to ask. Maybe that says something about me.

The sun sinks lower, stretching shadows long across the cracked earth. Derrick slows, scanning the area before nodding toward an overgrown ruin. "We camp here." It's the remains of an old building. The roof is half-collapsed, but the back wall still stands. It'll be enough to block the worst of the wind. We drop our packs, and I roll my shoulders, shaking the stiffness from my limbs. Derrick pulls out some more ration bars and tosses one my way, then starts on building a fire.

Above, the sky is a suffocating stretch of gray-green haze, thick with pollution and low-hanging clouds. I stare up, out of habit, searching for something I know isn't there. The fire is small, barely enough to chase back the dark, but it's ours. It's enough to remind me that life clings on even when the world says it shouldn't, so maybe I will too.

Questions tangle in my mind, winding tight like wires. I press my eyes shut, trying to push them away. The ground beneath me is too hard, too still. It doesn't move like the ship. Then something shifts. A strange bell chimes, and the air fills with the murmur of voices. There is a sizzling noise, and something scraps against glass.

I open my eyes and I am not in the wasteland. Strange lights flicker overhead, buzzing like trapped insects. The walls are lined with polished chrome, and a counter lined with spinning stools. There is a distinct odor, something I don't have a name for.

A glass pot rests in my hand, filled with warm dark liquid, and I am wearing strange clothes. Where are my own clothes? I know this place, not from my life on The Raven, but somewhere quieter and sadder, where dreams die between shifts and the days bleed together. A life I almost remember. A life that isn't mine... but could have been.

A voice calls my name and I turn. Two people sit at the counter, a man and a woman. Their faces blur, not like fog, but like something trying to exist in two places at once. The light bends around them and the edges of their bodies flicker, as if they are only half here.

"She's waking up," the girl murmurs.

"Not yet," the boy says.

Who are they? Why does it feel like I know them? The room stretches, walls pulling away and booths warping like melted wax. I stare at my reflection in the glass. My face stares back, but it is not me. I am somehow softer. Weaker. The walls shudder, distorting like melting wax. Then the ground is gone. My scream rips through the air. My body twists, and for one terrible moment, I feel myself coming apart. A hand reaches for me, and I choke on thick air, my lungs seizing as I wake to Derrick's hands on my shoulders, shaking me.

"Skye."

I blink up at him, disoriented. The wasteland is back. The fire is still burning, the scent of smoke and dirt anchor me to reality. His hands are steady, but his eyes aren't. I see the helplessness. The kind that comes from loving something you don't know how to save. He exhales, relief flickering across his face. "You were having a dream. I couldn't wake you."

I swallow hard and my body trembles. Nightmares have haunted me before, but this wasn't a nightmare, it was something else. Something I don't think I was meant to remember.

CHAPTER 18

The Owl

The morning sun warms my face first, and when I open my eyes, steam rises from the ground, remnants of last night's rain. Muirenn and Micah are tending another small fire, and I wonder if they've slept at all. The rich smell of coffee seeps into the air, pulling me out of my hammock. I roll to my feet and join them. Muirenn hands me a blue camp cup filled with steaming liquid, and Micah tosses me a gas station muffin, the plastic already torn, like he knew I wouldn't refuse. It's such a small thing, but it roots me in this moment, where I am more than just a passing thought.

"You okay?" Micah asks, his brows knitting with concern. "That dream seemed rough."

"Yeah," I say through a mouthful of dry muffin. I take a sip of coffee to wash it down before continuing. "I've had night terrors and weird dreams for as long as I can remember." Muirenn and Micah exchange a look, and I'm reminded of last night's conversation. "Who are the First Ones?" I ask Muirenn.

They exchange a resigned look, like they'd been waiting for me to ask. If the question bothers her, she doesn't show it. Instead, she tilts her head, as if deciding how much to tell me. Finally, she speaks. "They're my ancestors," she says, then glances at Micah, correcting herself. "Our ancestors." Interesting. If she thinks I look like them, does that mean she believes we're related?

"You mean like indigenous people from Maine?" The words leave my mouth before I can stop them, and I regret it. I don't look anything like the people who were here first. If anything, I have the kind of pale, washed-out features that scream Viking heritage. Meanwhile, both Micah and Muirenn have dark hair, sharp features, and deep blue eyes that make my own pale irises feel almost translucent in comparison. They are striking. I am invisible.

"No," she says. "Our people weren't from here. They weren't even from where they lived." That's cryptic. Her gaze drops to my necklace. "Can I see it?"

I unfasten the clasp and hand it over. The pendant is the only piece of my past I have left. A last tie to a life I don't remember. Muirenn removes her own pendant and holds them side by side. Hers is close to a triskelion, while mine looks more like a distorted infinity symbol had a baby with a yin-yang. She studies them for a moment, then hands mine back.

"The sea caves are sacred to our people," she says. "I'm interested to see what you think."

I glance at Micah, trying to gauge his reaction. He seems like the logical, science-minded type. Less inclined to buy into spiritual talk. But he nods along with Muirenn, at ease.

He catches me watching him and grins. "My sister has taught me a lot about our people," he says. "I try to soak up as much as I can."

"We should get moving," Muirenn interjects. "We have limited time, and the tide can be dangerous."

I swallow hard. The reality of the sea cave, and the fact that it could be submerged if we misjudged the timing, lodges itself in my brain, sending unease through me. Part of me regrets wanting to go at all. But curiosity is louder than fear, so I shove the doubt aside and pack up my gear. I break down my hammock and sleeping bag, stuffing them into my pack.

"You can leave that in the Jeep. I'll lock it," Micah suggests. "I've got a daypack with water and snacks." I nod but, when he isn't looking, grab my cash and shove it into my bra.

The trail starts off winding through a thick stretch of pines and birches with an earthy scent. There is damp moss, and fallen leaves litter the ground. There are a few roots that jut out across the path, but otherwise, it's an easy climb. As we ascend, the trees thin, revealing glimpses of the ocean. The rhythmic crash of waves grows louder against the rocky cliffs below.

When we round a bend, the world stretches wide before me. The Atlantic is glittering beneath the morning sun, and light sprawls over the waves in molten gold. The ocean doesn't care if the world above it is falling apart. It still breathes, still sings against the cliffs. If something so vast can survive, maybe so can I. Farther out, the sea shifts and dark swells rise. It churns in a way that makes me nervous, though I can't tell if I'm imagining it or if some storm is brewing.

Micah stops beside me as he takes in the view. "Never gets old."

Muirenn is a few steps ahead of us, and she tilts her face toward the wind. "We are close," she says over her shoulder. "Let's keep moving."

The descent begins, and the path turns treacherous. The dirt gives way to uneven stone, smoothed by centuries of wind and waves. Each step must be placed carefully. To the left, the rocks are slick. One misstep, and you'd slide toward the edge where the cliff drops into the crashing waves below.

The air is cooler here, and the cave entrance waits in the distance, half-hidden in shadows, dark and yawning like the maw of some giant creature. I hesitate for just a second, then step through the mouth, tucking myself behind Muirenn.

Inside, the cave feels almost sacred. Salt clings to my skin, the damp cold threading through my clothes. The walls press close, yet the space feels vast as if something is waiting and watching. A carving marks the ground, its swirling design similar to Muirenn's triskelion. I crouch beside it, tracing my fingers over the grooves. I think the Wabanaki people were the first here. This land belongs to them. And yet, Micah and Muirenn seem tied to this place in a way I don't understand.

The air hums with energy. It prickles along my skin. Outside, the waves crash, the sound funneled through the cave's mouth,distorting into something that sounds like a mournful wail. Farther back, a narrow crevice cuts into the rock. Micah moves toward it without hesitation.

"How far back do these caves go?" I ask.

"Far," he answers, already slipping between the rocks.

I glance at Muirenn, trying to gauge how worried I should be. "When does the tide come in?"

She pauses, tilting her head as if listening to something beyond the waves. "Couple of hours at least." Then, she follows her brother into the dark. The cave suddenly feels smaller, and I hurry after them.

Muirenn hands me a flashlight, and I follow them deeper. The air grows stale and the cave walls glisten with seawater dripping down in thin rivulets. Beneath my feet, the stone is slick, and the echoes of the Atlantic pulse like a heartbeat through the tunnel.

Without warning, the tide surges. The wave slams into me leaving no time to think. Micah's voice cuts through the roar, but I can't reach him. Water yanks me off my feet and cold surges over my head, then retreats. Water crashes between us again, rising too fast. I lunge for a foothold, but the current yanks me backward. The cave is shifting, reshaping itself, and I have no control. Walls tighten as the water forces me into a narrow passage, and then there's no more ground beneath me.

I'm shoved forward, the force of the surge relentless. I kick, desperate to stay above water, but the current is stronger. My shoulder slams into a rock, pain bursting white-hot along my arm. Then I try to twist away, but the water yanks me under. My lungs seize as I plunge into the cold. Salt fills my throat. My limbs flail, but I can't tell which way is up. A rush of images explodes in my mind. The dream. Then, the world spits me out, launching me into open space.

I break the surface with a ragged gasp, convulsing as I suck in air. Water clings to my skin, but I'm alive. I scramble against slick stone, fingers digging into the rough edges, and I haul myself up. After blinking away the salt and fear, I take it all in. I am in a massive underground chamber. The walls arch high above, and a strange, unnatural glow flickers across the wet stone. My body trembles and the only sound I hear is water dripping.

"Micah! Muirenn!" I shout. The only answer is my voice, bouncing off the stone walls. I force myself to take a slow breath. Think, Skye. You can figure this out. I haven't done much spelunking, but common sense is common sense, and panicking will only burn through oxygen and energy.

Oh, shit. Oxygen. My pulse spikes. Am I going to run out of air? The thought slams into me, but I shove it away. No, we had time before the tide came in. Muirenn said a couple of hours. This had to be a rogue wave, some freak surge.

I close my eyes and focus on my breathing. In, out, slow, steady. There has to be another exit. Most caves have multiple openings. I remember reading something about a blowhole in the park. Could I be near it? My flashlight is long gone, but I'm not in complete darkness. The eerie glow clings to the stone, casting just enough light for me to see.

Then I feel a faint breeze against my skin and relief floods through me. Moving air means an opening. I scan the cavern, my eyes adjusting to the dim light. There is a wide passage where the ground slopes upward. Instinct screams that up is good. Higher ground means a better chance of finding an exit. I move toward it, careful with each step. The stone beneath my feet is dry. That's... odd. I glance down, expecting the slick sheen of saltwater. Nothing. Another few steps, and I can't hear the ocean anymore.

Did I somehow get turned around? Move too far inland? The glow along the walls intensifies. It's not just blue anymore, but has streaks of green with faint veins of something almost metallic. Then ahead, I see an archway. Not shaped by time or tide, but by human hands.

Through the archway, I step into a chamber that doesn't feel real. It's like some forgotten storage room in a museum, but wrong. Artifacts are scattered across the space. Some are placed with precision, others abandoned, half-buried under dust and time. My gaze catches on a tarp draped over something large, perhaps I can use it to float on if needed. I hesitate, then grip the fabric and yank it away.

A mirror. Its surface is clouded, but beneath the dust, I see my reflection. She looks like me, but she isn't. There's something off in the set of her shoulders, like she knows something I don't. I step closer, fingers trembling as I reach up to brush my hair out of my eyes. My reflection does the same. Then it tilts its head. I did not.

A scream rises in my throat, but it never escapes. The face that stares back narrows its eyes. She looks like the version of me I see in my worst dreams, not who I am now. Am I dreaming? Did I ever go to the caves at all? Or am I still trapped in an endless nightmare?

I fight to breathe, my childhood therapist's voice whispering from a memory buried deep. Take control of your dreams. I force myself to move. My hand lifts, reaching for the glass. My reflection mirrors me this time. But the hesitation in her eyes isn't mine. Our fingers hover just apart, the dust swirling between the threshold. She moves first, her fingertip pressing against mine, and the glass ripples like water.

CHAPTER 19

The Raven

The land shifts beneath my feet, subtle but wrong, like the ground itself can't decide whether or not to stay solid. I don't know why I ever thought coming down here was a good idea. At first, everything looks normal enough. The earth is cracked with the occasional brittle vegetation, and there is an old road so worn down it's really just a suggestion. But the further we walk, the more strange it feels. Now and then, I hear a whisper of conversation, the faint murmur of voices carried on the wind. I turn, expecting to see someone. But there's nothing. Just me and Derrick. Then there are the footsteps. Sometimes, I hear our own echo back at us as if bouncing off something that isn't there.

"It's worse than the last time I came through here," Derrick mutters.

"When was that?" I ask.

"Fifteen years ago, maybe?" He tilts his head, gaze drifting toward the sky like it might have the answer. "You were probably around five. I was still a kid." Something in his expression shifts.

I don't press. We walk in silence for a while before he speaks again. "It wasn't long after that visit that the village was abandoned. Most of them went south. The Raven had liberated the slave cities, and the rest of the survivors... just sort of gravitated there." I study him, searching his face for a hint of how he feels. Grateful for what my mother did? Or resentful?

Then I see what's left of the world. A land that can't sustain us. Maybe it would be better if we all just faded away. Too many people. Not enough of anything. The village comes into view, a skeletal husk in the dying light. A palisade leans at an odd angle, half-buried by sand and the inevitable pull of gravity. Jagged wooden spikes are splintered and rotting, and the scavenged metal plating has long since been stripped away.

The village flickers. One blink, and the bones of ruined walls are whole again, standing tall against the dying light. The watchtowers rise, the air thick with the scent of burning wood. Shadows move where people should be. Then they are gone leaving only the empty husk, silent and still..

My pulse stutters. I turn to Derrick, but he seems untouched by whatever I just saw. "Did you see that?" My voice is tight.

Derrick scans the horizon. "See what?"

Was that a memory? A ghost? "Nothing."

We pass through what was once the heart of the town. The homes are skeletal remains with roofs caved in, windows shattered, doors torn from their hinges or left to swing in the wind.

"Is there anything you want to see?" I ask. "Do your parents have a resting place?"

Derrick shakes his head. "There's nothing here for me." His face is unreadable, locked behind whatever walls he's built over the years. Without another word, he turns away, leading me past the ruins toward the winding path upward. "We can go back to town and shelter for the night in the old council building," he adds as an afterthought.

I follow him, and the land feels emptier than it should. The earth cracks under my boots, brittle grass clinging to life, but nothing moves. By the time we crest the ridge, the world has gone still. At least there won't be another dust storm.

Something doesn't feel right. The place where the airship crashed should be unmistakable. There should be a scar on the land or fractured trees, but there is nothing. Not even a depression in the ground. I climb down a ledge, scanning the ground. Derrick follows, his steps cautious, but I don't wait. The pendant at my throat feels warm. I touch it, and heat pulses against my fingertips, almost like it's alive.

Derrick calls to me from the path that leads down. "I'm sorry," he says. "I wish there had been answers." His voice cracks a little on the apology. He looks at me like he's been losing me long before I ever ran.

The frustration wells inside me and I drop to my knees and start digging, my bare hands clawing at the dry earth. For half a second, the grit beneath my nails feels familiar. Not from here. Another life flickers, another me, feet bare in warm soil. Then it's gone, swallowed by dust and rage. It's useless. I want to tear the truth from this place, force it to give me what it owes me. I want to scream until the world has no choice but to listen. Then a deep, splintering sound rolls through the land, and a low rumble follows.

My head snaps up. Across the ridge, Derrick's eyes meet mine. Then we both turn toward the North. The air shifts. A pressure builds in my ears, and a jagged wound splits across the horizon, swallowing the last light of day. Derrick moves first. I don't even register his shout before the ground lurches, the earth splitting beneath me. I have just enough time to see the terror in his eyes before he disappears.

"Derrick!" I lunge toward the spot where he stood, but the ground gives way beneath me and I am falling. Everything hits at once: fear, shock, the gut-wrenching loss. Beneath it all, rage burns the hottest. If I die now, there will never be answers. I will never be whole.

The air is ripped from my lungs as dirt and rock cascade around me. My hands claw at the crumbling earth, nails scraping raw. My fingers catch a root, a fleeting tether between life and the abyss then it snaps. Weightless and falling, the world swallows me whole. I slam into an outcropping, pain exploding up my side before I slide further. My body scrapes against the walls and the ground vanishes beneath me again. For a heartbeat, I am weightless - then impact. Not solid rock, but a thick layer of debris. Dirt and detritus explode around me in a choking cloud. Silence follows, broken only by the slow trickle of pebbles tumbling down unseen slopes. My chest heaves and dust burns my throat.

Where am I? How far did I fall? Is Derrick even alive? I push up, scanning for pain, for broken bones. There are bruises and cuts, but nothing deadly. I take a slow breath, letting my eyes adjust. I am in a massive underground cavern. The walls are jagged and slick with moisture. The dampness is strange. I reach out, pressing my palm against the rock to feel the liquid. Despite that, the air is stale. My fists clench. I don't know how far I have fallen, but I am not dying down here.

"Derrick!" My voice cracks, shattering the silence before it is swallowed by the cavern's endless expanse. There is no answer. Guilt twists inside me. Poor Derrick, who has spent his entire life orbiting mine, is probably dead because of me.

No. That is weakness, and weakness does not survive. Think, Skye. I force my mind to focus, studying the space. The cavern floor is too smooth. Not natural, which means there is a way out, and then I feel the whisper of a breeze. Relief surges through me. Moving air means an exit.

Ahead, an archway looms, its edges too precise to be natural. Beyond it, the tunnel slopes up toward higher ground. This is good. I push forward, hoping the path leads to where Derrick fell. The walls change as I walk. The rough rock gives way to something structured. Then, ahead, a shape forms in the dim glow. A doorway.

What the hell is this place? I step through. The room has stone pillars that stretch toward the ceiling, their design shaped by human hands. Scattered across the floor are artifacts, half-buried in dust. Some were placed with care, others abandoned and forgotten. A rusted blade. A cracked helmet. A book, so decayed it crumbles at the edges.

Nearby, something sits beneath a rotting tarp. I grab the fabric and yank it away. A mirror. The glass is thick with dust, but my reflection is still there, watching. I step closer, my reflection doesn't.

She stands still, watching. That isn't me. Am I dreaming? Did I even fall? Or am I still on the ridge, caught in the Rift, being swallowed whole?

I lift my hand, fingertips hovering just above the surface. But there is hesitation in her eyes, and it isn't mine. Our fingers hover inches apart. The dust swirls in the space between us. Enough waiting. Enough hesitation. I reach first.

My fingers slam against the glass, and the surface ripples like water, distorting her face as if she's trapped behind it. A flicker of fear crosses her face but it's too late. I grip the reflection and pull. The glass shatters inward, shards dissolving into nothing as I yank her through.

INTERLUDE

Gemini

I am the daughter of ruin,
of rust, of broken wings.
I have swallowed the dust of dying gods
and risen with their bones in my hands.

I am not soft.
I do not kneel.

I am the daughter of silence,
of forgotten names.
I have stood at the edge of the world
and no one sees me fall.

I am the pause between breaths,
the echo swallowed by the wind.

My veins are rivers,
my ribs are roots,
my breath is wildfire.

I will not be tamed.

The sky-daughter howls,
wind-torn and wanting.
The ground-child snarls,
fists clenched, teeth bared.

I am not the girl they wanted.
I am not the girl they lost.
I am the ember in their ashes.
I am the scream in the wind.

I am something older.
Something wilder.
Something free.

I open my eyes.
And the world shudders.

PART 3

The Only Way Out is Through

WOLF GROVE MEDIA, LLC

CHAPTER 20

A scream splits my mind and ricochets inside of my skull. It's only when the echo fades that I realize the voice is my own. I'm sprawled on the ground and my body feels like it's been shattered and forced back together. My shoulder aches, as if the limb isn't my own. Because it isn't, is it?

You have never been whole, a voice whispers inside me. I don't have time for this. I sit up, my breath shuddering, and assess my situation. As soon as I am upright a tsunami of emotion crashes through me. Faces flicker in and out, loved ones and strangers jumble together, and memories shift like sand beneath my feet.

Where am I? Is this Maine? No, it must be The Broken Lands. I recognize the bitter taste of ash in the air. Derrick. I have to find Derrick. Does he even exist? And Micah? Muirenn? Panic surges in my chest. I hear my mother's voice warning me never to show weakness. Mira's voice. No. My mother and father are in Portsmouth, aren't they? My pulse pounds in my ears, and I shake my head, desperate to untangle one reality from another.

Who am I?

Pain dulls as my vision clears. The room I am in is filled with dusty shelves, shattered artifacts, and pieces of a world long past. I remember stumbling from the sea into this abandoned storage room, wondering if I'd wandered into some forgotten museum. A brittle laugh escapes me as I take it all in. Movement flickers in the corner of my vision, and I spin around. A person. The form shimmers in and out, flickering like a radio frequency caught between two signals, or a ghost lost in time.

Their skin is paler than mine, and silvery hair drifts as if suspended underwater. Our eyes meet, his widening in shock, mirroring my own confusion. Before I can speak, his form dissolves again, leaving nothing but empty air. He phases back, clearer this time and reaches toward me. Goosebumps prickle across my skin, and my heart leaps into my throat. He fades again, this time leaving only shadows.

From somewhere distant comes the echoing cry of a child. I whirl toward it, but the sound slips through my grasp. Was it real, or just another phantom haunting my fractured mind? This time the man doesn't return. I stand there, adrenaline racing beneath my skin and I've never felt so alive.

My existence still feels wrong, but I refuse to spend the rest of my life moldering away in some dusty storage room. In truth, nothing about my motivations has changed: find a way out, get my bearings, and deal with whatever awaits me next.

The mirror still sits in the middle of the room. For a brief moment, I considered touching it again. Perhaps it could put everything back the way it was. Something inside recoils at that thought. I've learned enough to know that "the way it was" could be wrong. With a shudder, I turn away and head back toward the doorway.

Outside, the walls pulse with a strange energy I did not notice before. It's like I've gained some new sense. If I squint just right, there are strands shimmering in all shades of colors. Color is a clumsy word, but there's no good way to describe them. I reach out, tracing one of the brighter threads with my fingertips. Then I follow it, drawn forward by instinct, until the cave gives a rumble. The tunnels groan around me, and the stone beneath my feet shifts, a warning I realize too late. My heart leaps into my throat as I lift one cautious foot, and then the ground opens beneath me.

Gravity pulls at me, and for one terrifying heartbeat, my stomach drops. I flail, grasping at nothing but empty air as I teeter at the edge. Then, my balance returns, and I stagger backward, heart hammering. "Well," I mutter, glaring down into the blackness below, "that was definitely the wrong way."

Before choosing another path, I pause, struck by the sheer absurdity of my own calm acceptance. The caves shift, rearranging themselves like stubborn puzzle pieces, and here I am, unbothered. I must be in shock, or losing what little remains of my mind. With a resigned sigh, I turn around and pick a new direction, hoping this one won't try to kill me.

The air in the caves doesn't smell right, it is full of memory, things lost and things yet to come. Voices drift up, distorted as if filtered through layers of reality. I can't tell if they belong to anyone I know, but hearing them sparks something inside me. Hope, maybe. At least it means there's more life here than just me and the ghost haunting these god-awful caves.

Wait. If this is real, and they're real, then why do my memories feel like smoke slipping through my hands?

I slow my pace as I approach a bend in the tunnel, wary of the ground falling out from beneath me... literally or figuratively. Hope and caution war inside me, but then Micah's familiar laugh cuts through, echoing off the cave walls. I linger in the shadows, holding back, and listen before I move closer.

"Any sign of her?" Micah asks, sounding worried. "How could we have been so stupid?"

"It wasn't time," Muirenn answers. "The way should have been closed. It should have just been a cave."

"Well, clearly you were wrong," Micah snaps back. I freeze, expecting to feel relief at hearing Micah's voice.

"I'm never wrong," Muirenn replies with a voice as sharp as a knife. Then her voice softens. "There's something about that girl that isn't right." My heart sinks. She's talking about me. I should be angry, but instead, something inside me agrees.

"Don't say it like that," Micah sighs. "If she heard you, it'd crush her."

It does.

"No, I just mean she doesn't fit in that world," Muirenn clarifies. "I felt the same way about you when we first met."

Enough. Whatever they thought of me, it sounded like they could help me escape this mess and maybe even find Derrick. My heart aches at the thought of him. What had I dragged him into? And what if Micah and Muirenn weren't as safe as I'd first believed? Regardless, debating myself in this endless dark was getting me nowhere.

"Hello?" I call out, stepping forward. "Micah? Muirenn?"

"Skye!" Micah shouts, rushing forward to sweep me into a bear hug.

His hug is too much, too fast, and both versions of me recoil. The Skye from Earth hates it, too much familiarity that has not been earned. The Raven's daughter doesn't trust it. What if it's a trick, and he is trying to contain me? I force myself to endure it, stiff as a corpse in his arms.

Micah pulls back, frowning as he studies me. I force a smile that feels foreign on my lips. "You're okay?" he asks, still watching me.

"I... yes," I say, a beat too late. "A little water never hurt anyone."

"We should get back before the tide comes in," Muirenn says, her gaze fixed on me as if expecting me to elaborate on my experience. When I don't, she turns and begins walking. "This way."

I trail behind her, eyes and ears alert for any sign of Derrick. For now, it's best to play my cards close. As we round a bend, the distant sound of the ocean fills the cavern. "I could have sworn I came this way earlier, when I was looking for you," I try to gauge her reaction and she flicks her wrist dismissively.

"It's easy to get turned around if you don't know these caverns."

"Wait," I say, remembering. "I need to know if Derrick survived, or at least find what's left of him."

Micah and Muirenn exchange confused looks. "Who's Derrick?"

Derrick would be utterly lost in a world so full of oceans and open skies. Yet now I'm beginning to question whether The

Broken Lands were just a figment of my imagination. But no, that world was far too real to have been just in my head. Still, what if these two start thinking I'm losing my mind?

"I must have hit my head harder than I thought," I mutter. "I thought I heard a man's voice. I... don't even know where that name came from."

"It was probably just Micah," Muirenn replies a little too quickly. "The acoustics in here are strange."

I whisper a quick prayer to the wind, hoping Derrick has found somewhere safe. For a heartbeat, the air stirs, and I freeze. Coincidence? Or something deeper? A small laugh escapes my lips. Lena's influence, I think, but deep down, part of me wonders if the wind answered. Shaking myself from these thoughts, I follow the twins back into the sunlight, and before I know it, we're at the Jeep again.

"We should get you to a hospital," Micah says, turning on the engine.

"No - " I say, sharper than I intended. For once, I'm not handing my broken pieces over to strangers. I'm not a project. I'm not anyone's ward. Softening my tone, I add, "Let's just go grab something to eat. And maybe something for this headache."

"You're the boss," he says. Since when? I wonder. I hadn't even planned on traveling further with them; Acadia was supposed to be the end of the line. We pull into a shopping center, spotting a Friendly's at the far end.

"I'll grab you some Advil from the drugstore," Micah says with a reassuring smile.

I follow Muirenn into the restaurant, and we slip into a booth. I notice a newspaper left behind by a previous customer and pick it up absentmindedly, scanning the headlines. My heart stops as a headline catches my eye:

Portsmouth Woman Presumed Dead After Disappearing in Acadia National Park

Beneath the bold print is my own face staring back at me. My breath catches as I pull the hood of my sweatshirt tighter to cover my distinctive hair. My pulse races as I glance at the date printed at the top - September 26th.

That can't be right. It was still August when I left home. How much time have I lost?

Hands trembling, I force myself to focus on the article, reading on in disbelief.

Portsmouth, NH *- Skye Hartwell, twenty-two-year-old Portsmouth resident, is presumed dead following her disappearance in Acadia National Park, Maine, authorities announced yesterday.*

Hartwell was last seen leaving The Friendly Toast in downtown Portsmouth on August 28. Family members stated she was embarking on a brief solo trip to Maine, something she'd mentioned previously to close friends and relatives. According to her parents, Dr. Jonathan Hartwell and Margarat Hartwell, Skye had planned regular check-ins during her trip. "This is completely out of character for her," Margaret Hartwell said. "She was always diligent about checking in, always responsible."

Maine authorities confirmed that Hartwell arrived at Acadia on August 29. A park ranger located her hammock and belong-

ings near one of the sea caves, where a significant ocean event occurred later that evening.

"Given the evidence found at the scene, we believe Ms. Hartwell may have been exploring the sea caves when the waves struck unexpectedly," said Ranger Daniel Collins of Acadia National Park. "Unfortunately, these caves are extremely hazardous at high tide."

Despite extensive searches by park rangers and Maine Marine Patrol, no body has been recovered, and search efforts have been scaled back after several weeks with no new findings.

Hartwell's disappearance marks the latest in a series of incidents in the area over the past decade. In 2016, another young hiker, Matthew Brennan of Bangor, disappeared in a similar fashion near the same caves. Additionally, three fatalities have been recorded since 2010 involving visitors swept into the sea during tidal surges. Park officials strongly urge visitors to remain vigilant around coastal cave areas and heed all posted warnings.

The Hartwell family held a private memorial service last weekend. "We're devastated, but holding onto hope," Dr. Hartwell stated. "We just want to bring her home."

Authorities ask that anyone with additional information regarding Skye Hartwell's disappearance contact Acadia National Park officials or the Maine State Police tip line.

Micah returns with a bottle of Advil and tosses it my way. I catch it, pop two, and swallow dry. My eyes stay locked on the newspaper.

This world thinks I'm dead. In a way, I am. I will never be that girl again and nothing would ever be the same. Good riddance. This place never wanted me, anyway. But that's the daughter of

The Raven talking. I reach for the pendant tucked beneath my shirt. My fingers trace its shape. Maybe I'm dead to them, but here, in this heartbeat, I still exist. The truth is, flawed as they were, the people I touched only ever did the best they could. It was never their job to save me or their responsibility to make me feel wanted or needed.

Micah laughs as he chats with Muirenn about pastries, but the words blur, dissolving into the background.

"Skye?" Muirenn's voice is cautious.

"Yeah." I force a smile. "I just… forgot what it was like to feel."

"It's been a month since we went into the cave, you know." I say, pushing the newspaper toward them.

Micah exhales. "For real?" He doesn't look surprised.

I narrow my eyes. Why doesn't he look surprised? Muirenn doesn't blink. Then, her lips curl into something knowing.

"It's time for some hard truths," she says, matter-of-fact. I nod, but inside I already know the hardest truth. I'm not sure who I am anymore, or where I belong.

CHAPTER 21

Back in the Jeep, I sink into the back seat and wish I could vanish into the upholstery. It's strange that after all those years of wanting nothing more than to be seen, now all I want is to disappear. For a heartbeat, I'm back on that fateful day riding in my parents' Subaru to my new home. They kept repeating that everything will be okay, like if they say it often enough, it might make it true. I wonder if they now blame themselves, even a little, for me going "missing."

We are just sitting there in the parking lot and Micah twists around in the driver's seat to catch my eyes. "This is going to be a lot."

I give a weak laugh. "More than getting swept away in a sea cave and..." Then my throat closes around the rest. I'm not ready to face the part about what happened after the cave, or what I've become.

Micah doesn't push. "The first time I realized the universe was bigger than all this," he says. "I was about twelve or thirteen. It was summer, and we'd just moved. Everything was changing in my life." Muirenn snorts from the passenger seat. It isn't loud, but I catch the flick of an eye-roll in the rearview mirror. She's probably heard this story a thousand times. "That was also the time I found out I had a twin," Micah continues..

"Wait - what?" I sit up straighter. For a second, it sounds like something out of The Parent Trap.

"Yeah. A lot of weird stuff happened fast. Turns out, the world we know isn't... singular. There are a lot of others. Dimensions, maybe?" His voice wavers as though he's half-questioning himself, but the way he watches me says he's more concerned about whether I can follow his train of thinking. "These places are stitched together. Layers of reality. Sometimes, the seams slip, and people... slip through."

My stomach drops. The dreams. My life on The Raven. I'm not sure if I've fallen, or crashed, or been thrown through.

Muirenn tilts her head. "It's not always falling. If you learn, you can make it happen. There is this whole group of people that just wander through time. We call them the First Ones, but they may not have been first at all." It sounds cryptic, but catches my interest. At one point, they had compared me to one of these first ones. I lean forward.

"Don't get ahead," Micah interrupts.

"It may be behind," Muirenn shoots back with a grin. I have not seen her this animated, and it's a rare moment where they seem like actual siblings.

Micah ignores her and goes back to his story. "I tried to run away that summer, but where I ended up wasn't here. It's this... space between things. Not a world or a void exactly, more like a threshold. A place that's always becoming, but never quite is. I don't think people are meant to live there, but some do."

He shoots a glance at Muirenn. "I think we're like antibodies, caught in the bloodstream of something bigger." His words give me a chill. "The place where I ended up kind of sits outside of time, and the caves we explored are an entry point that connects to it."

My mouth goes dry. "You said it's outside of time?"

"That's one way to put it. With time, there isn't a straight line. It's more like a chord in music. Everything resonates at once, but not." Helpful. Muirenn makes a small sound, but doesn't interrupt. "Have you ever heard of brane theory?"

"I've heard of brain freeze," I mutter.

He grins, but he gets a wild look in his eyes. It's the look people get right before they launch into something they are very passionate about. "So, okay. Imagine our universe is a piece of paper. That's a 'brane.' Short for membrane. Now, imagine tons of these branes floating in higher-dimensional space. Physicists call this the 'bulk.' We only ever perceive our own sheet. But sometimes, "these branes... they brush against each other. And when that happens, weird things bleed through. Energy, gravity, matter. Sometimes... people."

His hands make vague shapes in the air, like he could scoop the ideas out and hand them to me. "My theory?" He shrugs. "Isdralan might be unique. Part of the bulk - "

"Isdra-what?"

"That's where I grew up," Muirenn cuts in. "Where Micah went. It's a bit more... magical than here."

Micah glances at her and smiles. It's almost condescending. "When I ran away as a kid, I ended up in Isdralan by accident. Or maybe not by accident, but... doesn't matter." His voice flattens a little, less smug. "Anyway. I think Isdralan is the connective tissue between realities. Explains the unpredictability. Gravity shifts. Time loops. Echoes. All of it."

"Okay, okay." I hold up a hand. "You're losing me. I have a headache, and you're throwing branes and gravity and - " I wave. "Paper? - at me like we're watching a documentary."

He leans back. "Fair."

"But just to be clear," I say, "you're saying I fell into the glue between universes?"

"That's one way to put it."

"Some people fall," Muirenn murmurs. "Others... are drawn."

"And somehow... a whole month passed in a few hours?" My voice sounds too small.

Micah's smile twitches. "Could be. Or maybe not. Hard to say when the rules don't exist the way we think they do."

I sag against the seat. There are too many questions, and I can't ask them. Not without unraveling everything. "So, Muirenn." My voice comes in a whisper. "If you grew up in this Isdralan place, and him too, why are you still the same age?"

Muirenn gives me a lopsided grin, a mirror of Micah's, then shrugs. "I age well?"

"No rules," Micah offers, deadpan.

"Okay." I sigh. It's supposed to be frustration, but it comes out more like a whimper. No use pretending. I need them. I need them like a drowning person needs the shore.

So I tell them. Everything. The cave. The mirror. The man who flickers. The impossible thing where I am two people, somehow. Leaving Derrick behind, not knowing if he's even alive. How I feel like I'm stitched together wrong now. Pulled between too many places. The people I love here. A world I didn't even know existed until maybe an hour ago. And then, the kicker, another world out there needing saving, and somehow it's supposed to be me.

It's too much.

And I tell it all too fast. Words stumble out in a mess. No breathing space between them. The kind of story that sounds like lying, but it's not. It's just fear trying to outrun itself. My mouth won't stop. I know how I sound manic, like if I just say it fast enough, it'll make sense, or better yet, go away.

But they just... listen. Like it's nothing they haven't heard before. When I finally shut up, Muirenn only reaches out and rests a hand on my shoulder.

That tiny gesture cracks me open like an egg. I don't cry pretty. No glittering tears or quiet sobs. It's snotty and loud and awful. I make a sound I'm pretty sure only dying goats are supposed to make, and once it starts, it won't stop.

They never look away. Micah's voice is soft. "You're already through the first door. The next part... it's never easy. But you don't belong to just one world anymore."

Muirenn nods once. "You're whole, when you were not. That changes everything."

When my outburst is over, we sit in silence until I break it. "I don't know what to do."

Micah pulls up the paper, glancing at my article. "Sounds like there may be a memorial. What if we head that way, and you can figure it out as we go?"

I give a snuffle and nod. "I like that..."

We drive in silence, the road unspooling ahead of us like a thread we can't rewind. When we arrive, Micah guides the Jeep into the parking lot of the beach club just south of Jenness. It is strange we get there at just the right time, but I roll with it. There's already a group gathered, clustered near the edge of the dunes, and the wind whips the dry grasses sideways.

They wait in the car while I push the door open and step outside. The cold slaps me in the face like it knows what I'm about to do. Sand shifts under my boots as I step out, pulling my hoodie up tighter, like it might still hide me, and approach the small crowd standing in the rear. Here in the back, I am surrounded by people I don't recognize. A single raven watches from the driftwood fence, dark against the gray sky. Its head tilts like it knows me.

It isn't a funeral, that much is obvious. The Hartwells were never big on ceremony or religion, but there's an air to it that is reverent. A remembrance, maybe. Still, I'm shocked by the crowd. More people than I expected. Closer to the front, I spot most of the Sunshine Diner staff, people who barely noticed me when I worked there. There are classmates from high school and college too. All sorts of faces I recognize more from background noise than from actual friendship, but they're here, looking appropriately somber.

And then there's Rhu and Vi. They're easy to find, standing apart but still surrounded by a few locals who are just pretending to care. Rhu's face is pinched, but I know her well enough to see the exhaustion leaking through. Vi has one arm around her, scanning the group like she's daring someone to say the wrong thing.

Seeing them is like catching a punch I don't see coming. Guilt is written all over Rhu's face as she steps forward. Part of me wants to comfort her, and tell her none of this is her fault, the other is giddy with the knowledge she knows if she had followed through, this wouldn't have happened.

She brushes a strand of hair from her face, and her voice carries against the wind. "Skye was the embodiment of her name. She shifted like the weather: stormy, sunny, never still. You'd think she was a chameleon, but it was always her. Never someone you could hold on to. Quicksilver. But we loved her."

A single tear escapes before I can stop it. It's almost funny how in death, Rhu understands me better than she ever did in life. I scan the crowd. Most people wear polite, practiced grief. Only the Hartwells, Rhu, and Vi seem to carry something heavier, something real. But even their grief is for someone I can't claim to be anymore. They mourn the girl who belonged here. I'm not sure I ever did. I realize that's okay. Maybe grieving who I was is part of making space for who I'm becoming, and I can carry the ache without letting it anchor me. Somehow, I know The Broken Lands still remembers me, perhaps that's why nothing ever fit here the way it was supposed to.

Then there is this place called Isdralan... maybe that's the only place that gets me out of this limbo. Micah called it the bulk - but I think I am right in thinking it's more like glue. Glue is what I need right now, to piece together whatever it is I am. The Broken Lands couldn't tell me. Earth never could. If there's an answer, it's waiting beyond that threshold. There is also Derrick. The thought of him wandering the caves, thinking he had lost me, would crush him.

My fingers find the pendant before I even think to reach for it. The one the Hartwells said they found with me, and Lena said was my real mother's. It's stupid, but it felt like proof I existed, even if no one else noticed. I turn back to the Jeep and climb in the back seat.

Micah catches my eye. "Ready?"

I glance one last time at the raven perched on the dunes. It watches me, solemn and still, like it's given its blessing. A gust stirs the dry grasses, tugging at my hoodie. I wonder if it's the same wind that Lena listens to, or maybe it's her way of telling me I'm not alone.

"I've got my closure," I say. Micah tilts his head, wanting to ask more. But he just nods instead. This time, when I turn away, I don't look back.

CHAPTER 22

We're almost back to Acadia before I speak. I spend most of the ride just soaking in the world around me. This place has been my home for seven years, yet under this bright blue sky, everything feels new. For a moment, I'm tempted to stay. It's safe here with plenty of food and decent protection. Even the idea of going back to school sounds appealing.

That's the daughter of The Raven talking. She can blend in, keep growing, and find real freedom if she wants. Meanwhile, in The Broken Lands, I matter. Hell, I'm the Child of Prophecy there, and I'm starting to suspect that title might be more accurate than either The Owl or The Raven ever realized.

"I need to go back to the caves," I say at last.

Muirenn starts at the sound of my voice, one eyebrow lifting. "There are easier ways to pass between worlds," she points out, glancing skyward. "Conveniently, the fall equinox is coming up, and I can take us straight to Isdralan."

If only it were that simple. The thought of skipping the caves feels wrong on a bone-deep level. "I left Derrick behind in the collapse," I tell her, voice tight. "I have to go back the way we came."

Micah's expression darkens. "The caves are dangerous. You can get trapped in a loop forever. There are fates worse than death." He shudders, like he's remembering something he wishes he could forget.

"If you can just get me there, I'll go alone," I say. "I'm not expecting either of you to come."

"Fah - " Micah starts, then snorts. "You're not going in alone. I'm going, too."

"Me too," Muirenn adds.

Before I know it, we're driving down the same road we did just days before. It seems like it has been a lifetime - two, to be more precise. Having two sets of memories is exhausting, especially when they create conflicting goals. Micah pulls the Jeep into the same place as before, and the wind outside smells of the sea and damp earth. It's a familiar smell, having lived on the coast for so long. It is contrasted with having the ocean be a new experience. There is no smell of sulphur and death in the air.

It's dusk when he parks, but the trailhead is easy to spot. I climb out first, stepping onto the gravel. The gulls overhead screech like they're warning us to stay away. I can't. Not when Derrick might be down there.

"I would be safer to wait until morning," Micah suggests.

I ignore him and start down the path. He and Muirenn exchange a glance before trailing me, but it feels right that I'm in front. Something in my bones knows Derrick is down there waiting for me. Memories from The Broken Lands flicker in my mind: I've navigated storms and rifts more dangerous than anything these tunnels can throw at me - I hope.

Fortunately, the tide is out, leaving ribbons of seaweed clinging to the rocks as we enter the cave. Without a word, I click on my flashlight, and the pale beam skims the dripping walls. Micah and Muirenn follow close on my heels. With each step, the roar of the waves fades behind us until the only sound left is our own breath echoing off the stone walls. The thin thread of light glints off the cavern walls as we push deeper.

"Derrick?" I call, and my voice echoes, sounding hollow and distant. The darkness feels alive, swallowing each scrape of my boots as I trudge forward.

"Be careful," Micah murmurs. "These tunnels shift. They can get treacherous in a heartbeat."

"I'm good," I say, remembering how the sky in The Broken Lands could twist on a dime. More than once, The Raven had to steer away from rifts when the clouds went that gray green color. It's strange having two sets of memories - one from Portsmouth, another from a place where storms swallow entire cities.

Eventually, the twins' voices fade, so I slow down.

"Derrick! Are you out there?"

You out there?

The voice that called back isn't my own. He is alive! His voice sounds weak, like it hasn't been used in forever, but I imagine he is starving and possibly hurt.

"I'm here!" I shout, speeding up my pace again.

I'm here...

A faint voice echoes up ahead.

"I'm coming!" I shout.

I'm coming...

"No, you stay there!"

Stay there... he agrees.

My heart leaps and I break into a run.

"Skye, slow down!" Muirenn calls from behind. "It's not safe!"

Not safe...

I hear Derrick's voice over my right shoulder, too faint to be real. I skid sideways, chasing that sound.

"Stop, Skye!" Micah cries

Skye... comes the echo, right behind me.

I spin around, pulse thrumming. "Derrick?"

A shape slides through the tunnel, pale as bone with features smudged by the half-light. Where is he going?

"I'm right here." I say.

Right here...

Something in the air prickles. My instincts scream, this is wrong, but hope hammers in my veins. I'm led into a narrower tunnel and desperation surges. Even if it isn't Derrick, no one should be trapped down here alone. When I round the bend, the ground drops away into a yawning chasm. A silhouette hovers on the far ledge, sad eyes boring into mine. Not Derrick. I am so close I can hear its heartbeat. Or is that my own?

"It's going to be okay," I whisper, terrified any louder noise will shatter the poor thing. My chest aches with a loneliness that can't be mine, but I feel it anyway. I inch closer, arm extended.

"Just hop over. I've got you."

I've got you...

The being pauses and meets my gaze. Its limbs stretch toward me, unnaturally long. The face is little more than a suggestion. I can't look away, and I feel it latch onto that ache I've carried and the loneliness I thought I'd buried. The ground crumbles beneath my feet and the cavern floor disappears in one dreadful second. I cry out as my balance gives, and the void devours my scream.

Then a hand locks around my arm, Micah's. His grip is like iron catching before I plummet. He yanks me back with a stran-gled grunt, and we collapse to the rocky floor. Across the gap, the creature remains silent and hollow-eyed.

Before I can speak, Muirenn skids up behind us. She sets a hand on my shoulder, eyes flicking from me to the figure in the darkness. "Don't let it lure you again," she warns, her voice low. "You won't escape twice."

I shudder, pressing close to Micah as the thing tilts its head, eyes brimming with hunger, then fades into the deep shadows beyond. We stay that way, the three of us huddled at the edge of the chasm, until we are sure it's gone.

"What was that?" I whisper.

"This place borders many worlds," Muirenn says. "Some creatures get lost here. Others..." She pauses. "They hunt." I stare into the darkness and wonder if it's still there, waiting for me, and resist the urge to try to follow. "It reads your sorrow," she warns. "If it catches you, it burrows into your mind, feed-ing on every hollow space you've tried to hide. We call them Soul-Eaters. They hollow you out until you're nothing but a voice that never stops calling."

Despair creeps in and I can't tell if it is the creature, or if I'm just never going to find Derrick. "What do I do now?" I mutter under my breath.

"Trust yourself," Micah says with a half-shrug. He looks like he wants to help, but he's clueless about how this place really works. I let out a bitter laugh. They seem so informed, yet deep down, they know less than I do.

"You pretend to know it all, but don't even know how this place works," I accuse.

Muirenn shoots me a sharp look. "It's not like that," she tries to explain. "Here, you have to trust your instincts. That's where I do my best. Micah lives in his head, but we've got all the time in the world." She tosses her brother a playful wink.

I'm fed up with cryptic nonsense, but somehow her confidence makes me feel like a child again. She reminds me a little of Lena. "If you're so experienced, why not lead us?" I snap.

She arches an eyebrow. "I could easily take us to my home. I know that route like the back of my hand. But if you want your friend, you'll have to lead. Stop trying to find him. Just... go to him."

"But I don't even know where to start!" I protest. I inhale, steadying myself. The tunnel ahead forks in two directions. Down one path, an old man perches on some bizarre throne. What the hell?

Micah tenses beside me. "Not that one..."

Closing my eyes, I force myself to breathe. A faint whiff of sulfur drifts past. It has the same smell as at home after a storm. "This way," I say at last.

My feet feel like they're wading through water, yet adrenaline keeps me moving. The air gets drier, and I am reminded of home. Then, I spot it. Derrick's leg protruding from a mound of shattered stone. He's alive! He's moving! My heart nearly explodes with relief.

Dust stings my eyes as I scramble over the debris. Each broken slab scrapes my palms, but I barely notice the pain. Micah grunts beside me, leaning his full weight into a heavy chunk of sandstone. It won't budge at first. I grit my teeth, forcing my body against it until, finally, it shifts with a dull scrape.

Derrick coughs, the sound like music to my ears. The rattling in his chest makes me want to cry and cheer all at once. We pry loose a slab pinning his torso, and he gasps, lungs protesting the sudden flood of air. He looks so normal. After everything that's happened, he is still just Derrick. In that moment, everything narrows down to him and the rise and fall of his chest. My relief is so fierce, it almost feels like pain.

He looks up into my eyes. "Skye," he rasps, voice raw, "I'm so sorry I couldn't keep you safe."

I laugh through the tears. "You idiot..."

He glances past me to Micah and Muirenn, confusion flickering on his face. Their fair skin almost matches mine, and Micah stands there, ready to haul Derrick up. "Where'd they come from?" Derrick asks, disoriented.

I hesitate. How do I explain the caves, the time lost, the worlds in between? "I, well, I met them after.... They helped me find you."

"Find me? I have not moved." He frowns, pushing himself upright with a grunt. "What happened?"

"Easy, friend." Micah grips his arm, steadying him.

"There was a rift storm," I say, choosing my words. "The ground collapsed. I thought we were done for. You must've blacked out."

Derrick rubs his eyes like no time has passed at all, while my heart aches with how much has changed. "I don't think I blacked out," he says. "The sun hasn't even sunk below the horizon yet." He tips his head toward the sky, confusion etched across his face. "We fell, then you found me... that was only minutes ago, right?"

A second bolt of green lightning rips through the churning sky, and thunder crashes so hard my teeth chatter. The ground buckles beneath us, threatening to hurl us into the gaping rift that looms just yards away. Derrick's grip on my hand tightens as hairline cracks creep across the dirt.

I clench my jaw, forcing myself to stay focused. There's a sense I can tap into, like Lena feeling the wind. Then I catch it: a low, humming energy in the air, vibrating through my bones. We have to move. Now. Micah and Muirenn scramble to our side, eyes darting between the storm above and the rubble surrounding us. Muirenn's lips press tight with worry as she scans the expanse.

"I do not know this place," she says. "You will need to get us back to the caves."

I nod, already pressing a palm against a fractured rock. There. A pulse tugging me like an invisible thread. It draws me toward a fissure in the ground. "Here!" I shout, the invisible pulse drumming in time with my heartbeat. Micah and Muirenn share a quick, uneasy glance, Muirenn's hand flying to something at her chest. Then they follow as I inch toward a narrow gap in the rocks.

"No way," Derrick rasps, trying to see past me. "That's a rift."

"It's not, trust me." I insist, giving him a firm shove. "Move!" I step in first. The ground seems to yield beneath me, but somehow I don't feel any fear, like the earth is guiding me.

"Hold her hand," Muirenn orders. Derrick slips his fingers through mine, and we descend together. Anxiety clenches my stomach, so I squeeze my eyes shut. By the time I open them, Micah and Muirenn have joined us, and we're back in the room with the mirror.

Micah's hand falls on my shoulder. "That sense of yours... did you have it before?"

I can only shake my head, exhaustion taking over. Muirenn helps Derrick steady himself, and I realize the storm is gone. For a few moments, none of us speak. At last, I inhale a shaky breath, dust coating my throat. "I don't know how I knew," I manage, voice trembling. "But thanks for pushing me."

Muirenn offers one of her rare smiles. "It worked. That's all that matters."

Derrick frowns. "But how did you do that?"

Muirenn smiles, looking more like a wise old crone than someone barely in her twenties. Tapping her abdomen, then me, and replies, "Sometimes, you just have to trust your gut."

CHAPTER 23

"Where are we?" Derrick narrows his eyes and inspects the room.

Micah's eyes wander too, curious about each object but careful not to touch. When he stands in front of the mirror, he pauses. "Wait!"

Although the surface looks black, his expression turns sad, as if remembering something. The mirror's surface ripples, a ghost-image of Micah flaring and then cracking like glass. He jerks back, and the mirror smooths itself out again.

"That's where my incident..." I trail off, not finishing my sentence.

It's Muirenn who draws my attention next. A nostalgic look settles over her face as she roams behind stacks of papers and shelves, as though she's expecting to find something. "I used to call this the relic room," she says to no one in particular.

"You've been here?" Micah asks, and she nods.

"I tried to run away once when I was younger." She eyes something that could be a statue or maybe just a hunk of driftwood. I honestly can't tell.

"What are you looking for?" I ask.

A blush colors her cheeks. "There was a person here who helped me find my way, spiritually, at least."

I stiffen slightly. I'd seen him too, flickering at the edge of the mirror room, half-faded like a forgotten story. Maybe we'd both found the same guide, only at different points in his unraveling. "Was he skinny?" I ask. "Stringy hair, about the same color as mine?"

She breaks into a smile. "You saw him?"

"Sort of," I answer. "He flickered in and out, like he was fading away."

"Oh..." She hesitates, and I can't quite read her expression. Then she shares her story:

"As I was growing up, I was lost and sad, and felt incomplete. This was long before I knew Micah existed. Our mother isn't exactly what you'd call warm. One day, I came across this room. The first time I saw him, I thought he was a statue. He was so still, and he barely seemed aware, even when I got close." I watch Muirenn trail her fingertips over a battered trunk, her gaze drifting to a place long past. "He spoke like poetry," she murmurs, eyes distant. "His eyes remind me of stars. He says time is an illusion, and that we've both been here forever. I like how his words feel like songs, and he likes how sharing his knowledge makes him feel alive."

While she talks, Derrick and I sift through a stack of relic crates. Dust dances in the stale air as I lift the lid on one, revealing a brass astrolabe. I brush away the grit and the gears spin on their own, as if drawn by some hidden magnet. Derrick leans in, the faint hum curling through our silence, but Muirenn's soft recollections still float around us like a half-remembered lullaby.

"He was tasked with guarding the relics. When I asked whose relics, he just said, 'the relics.' When I asked if they were dangerous, he only asked me what that meant. Honestly, it confused me as a child, but looking back, I don't think he'd spoken to anyone in a very long time." She pauses, smoothing her hand over a dusty shelf. "Anyway, he told me this room holds relics from our people's journeys. I found it strange at first because I didn't think he was the same as me, but maybe he was some kind of ancestor. Since then, Micah and I have learned that time isn't linear, even if our perception is."

I do my best to listen, but my mind spins in confusion.

"This room," Muirenn continues. "Is filled with history and knowledge from across the universes, if you know how to read it."

"Do you?" I ask.

"To an extent," she admits. "I came back often as a kid and visited him until one day he wasn't here anymore. He tried to teach me; I tried to learn. He invited me to become a relic keeper, but I didn't understand what that meant. I invited him to see the world. He said it had been too long, and he wasn't sure he knew how. After that, I never saw him again."

She steps closer to the mirror. "This mirror shows your true self, or takes you to your true self." Muirenn looks at me. "I think it put you back together the way you were supposed to be."

"Wait, what?" Derrick asks.

"I think that's for Skye to explain, if she wants," Muirenn says.

Derrick moves to my side and sets a protective hand on my shoulder. He still looks at me like I'm the same girl he promised to guard, not the shifting thing the world keeps trying to re-shape. Part of me aches for how simple he makes it seem.

"It's a long story. I'll share later," I promise him. I'm not sure how much I'm ready to reveal, but he deserves the truth. His whole life has revolved around me, and it's not fair. He should have a choice.

"There's another mirror in here that can help you travel to other dimensions," Muirenn adds, "but it has its own dangers. I guess everything in this place is risky in its own way." She glances at Micah, who looks sheepish.

"Yeah," he mutters. "I might've learned that the hard way."

Muirenn reaches for the amulet under her shirt. I think of my own and wonder if they're similar. When she pulls hers out, I gasp - it's shaped like a triskele, just like mine.

"Oh," I breathe, showing her my pendant in return.

She nods as though a puzzle has been solved. "Makes sense why you have one. Where did it come from?"

"It was found with me... both times."

"In Isdralan," Muirenn says. "My mother is what we call a Guardian. Micah and I will follow in her footsteps someday. They work with the cardinal directions - my mother is West. We each have these pendants. They're connected to time and how everything fits together, though Micah and I are still learning."

She motions to the tapestry on the wall, where bright stars and lines pulse like a living constellation. Muirenn plucks a single thread. Gravity lurches and books float, hair lifts, and every one of us staggers as if the floor has dissolved. A five-second micro-rift tears open, then slams shut with a crack that leaves the room spinning. The tapestry's glow flickers out, plunging everything into darkness. My question dies on my tongue, because in that moment, it's all too clear: this place is collapsing in on itself.

"Everything exists, and everything touches here," she says. "We're not meant to understand it all, but we try. Our ancestors, or our future progeny, do." A bright light begins to glow at the center. Smaller pinpricks of light expand around it. "They were closer to the center. To the light. As it grows, we move farther from the source. I think you might be closer to that center, like Micah and me."

"Why don't I know this?" I ask. Derrick has gone quiet, listening.

"Mira and Lena found you when you were just a baby," Muirenn explains, "but you were never truly theirs." Derrick looks at me, as though realizing how different we are.

"So... what do I do now?" If my people were travelers, maybe that's how I would save my world, only I can't remember the trick.

"You learn," Muirenn says. "The books here are cryptic, but in Isdralan, one of the other Guardians might teach you."

I picture The Broken Lands: the rifts yawning wider, and the ground buckling. Life on The Raven has sheltered me from how bad things are below. What happens when the rifts swallow everything? Will the sky still save us? What do we eat when there's no ground left to plunder? Across the room Derrick meets my gaze; he's running the same grim arithmetic.

"There isn't time," I whisper at last.

"You have all the time in the world," Muirenn replies with a careless shrug.

"Time means nothing," Micah adds, but the flicker in his eyes betrays him.

I round on him. "Easy for you to say. Maybe you can skip through seconds, but down there people are dying now."

Micah's shoulders sag. "Listen. Every outcome already exists. Success, failure, everything in between. We're not racing a clock; we're choosing which branch we stand on."

"Whether we see them or not, the other branches still happen." Muirenn adds.

"So somewhere there's a me who lets the world burn?"

"And another you who saves it twice over," Micah says. "All you can do is to nudge this branch the direction you want."

I look away, anger and grief knotting inside me, while Derrick stares at the floor already mourning the lives he can't reach.

"We can take you to someone you can learn from." Murienn adds. "It will help you to do everything you can."

For a heartbeat, I can't speak. Micah and Muirenn talk about splintered timelines as if lives are chess pieces, and every word makes my skin crawl. I need a way to keep the world from cracking in half, not a lecture on how my failure already "exists somewhere else."

I force my voice steady. "Is there anything here that can teach me?" If I can learn this, maybe I can fix something. Muirenn drifts to a bookcase, fingertips skimming battered spines until one seems to hum beneath her touch. She lifts it down, dust-free, and offers it.

I reach for it and my elbow brushes a stack of scrolls and they crash around us. Derrick snatches one before it hits the ground. For a heartbeat, nothing happens. Then I catch the shimmer of blue at the edge of my vision. I open my mouth to warn him, but it's too late: a cold flame sparks to life where his fingers make contact. His eyes go wider than I've ever seen them. With a strangled yelp, he hurls the scroll away. Blue embers trail through the air as it lands near my feet. I stomp it out as Derrick stamps on the rest, clumsy and frantic. My heart pounds so hard it rattles in my ribs.

I can still taste the ozone and old magic in the back of my throat, sharp as a blade. I want to say something clever, but all I manage is a shaky breath. The air thins, charged with the crackle of old magic. These weren't just relics. They bit back.

Muireen raises an eyebrow and ignores it. Typical calm that makes me want to scream. "This will get you started," she says. "But come to Isdralan with us. The Guardians there can guide you."

Across the room, Derrick meets my eyes and gives the tiniest shake of his head. Not safe. "Let me sleep on it," I say. "If time's really meaningless, we can spare one night."

Muirenn laughs, low and musical. "It isn't that simple. If I step out and return, I may find a different you, one who's lived months while I blinked."

Heat surges up my throat. I clamp it down and answer. "Then go."

Micah raises his hands, placating. "We'll stay till morning. Decide then."

"Fine." I snatch the book and retreat to the far end of the chamber. Derrick hesitates only a second before crossing to me. He pulls a dust-cloth from a marble statue and spreads it on the floor like a blanket, then sits beside me. His fingers brush my arm, lightning under my skin, and he flinches at the spark he feels too.

We open the tome. The script looks like knotted vines, yet the meaning blooms in my mind as if I've always known this language. Derrick tilts the page, baffled, and I realise he can't read a word. So I translate in a whisper, while Micah's and Muirenn's breathing slows into sleep on the other side of the hall.

The book is both map and riddle: the traveller carries the place of her birth in her marrow; follow that note and the world will answer. I can jump back to The Broken Lands, and because Derrick's bones were forged there too, I can pull him with me. It doesn't explain how to mend the rifts, but something deep in my ribs thrums you will know when the moment comes. I close the book, and tuck it in the pocket of my sweatshirt. "We have to go back," I breathe.

Derrick nods, jaw set. "I pledged my life to you the day Mira and Lena carried you home. I'll keep that vow until the day we die, whenever that is."

My heart splinters. He doesn't see how different we are, yet I can't bear to break his heart. "Thank you," I whisper, and press my lips to his. He shivers, but does not pull away.

Across the room, Micah and Muirenn sleep on, oblivious. I lace my fingers with Derrick's, feel the echo of The Broken□Lands tugging at me, and picture home: cracked earth, poisonous sky, and all the people still waiting. Hold on, I tell him without words. Then I let the world slip.

I grip Derrick's hand in the dark, pulse thunder in my ears. No fancy runes, no incantations, just a single breath and a gut-churning leap of faith. A noise behind us: a sudden scrape of wood. I lock eyes with him, heart pounding like it might burst. There's no going back.

We slam onto cracked clay under a night sky streaked green. My knees jar. Sirens wail in the distance. Derrick doubles over, retching from the dimensional whiplash. I stoop beside him, bracing a hand on his shoulder. Then it hits me and I can already feel the rift-quake rumbling in my bones. We have to move fast.

CHAPTER 24

We hit hard. Pain knifes up my ankle, and my leg wobbles under me like a snapped gear. Derrick, of course, tucks into a perfect roll and comes up on one knee. Show-off. I grit my teeth, test the foot, and stand, just as Derrick's expression drains from cocky to horrified. "I'm fine," I snap, already tired of being fussed over. He doesn't answer. He only lifts a hand and points.

We've landed in the same blasted clearing where the airship first crashed, but everything beyond it is gone. The distant skyline and bones of half-buildings where my mother and Lena grew up have been scraped flat. From horizon to horizon stretches a desert fissured by dozens of rift-storms that crackle and spit green lightning. I can almost feel the voids yawning beneath the crust, hungry.

How long were we gone? Did the world finish dying while we chased answers? Instinct dragged me back here, but it might have misfired. I picture Portsmouth's beach. Taste the tang of salt, and hear gulls wheeling overhead. For one reckless heartbeat I want to haul Derrick through there, find a quiet life, pretend this world is somebody else's problem.

But if The Raven shattered this realm, its last echo is standing in my boots. Whether or not I'm the child of prophecy Lena created, I'll be the one who decides what happens next. A single tear slips down my cheek. Earth can wait. First, we find out if this world still has a pulse.

I seize Derrick's hand. "Come on. Let's see if anyone's left."

He stares at the wasteland, voice hoarse. "The way's gone, Skye. Nothing could survive out there."

"Then we don't go that way," I say, forcing my words. "We skirt it, figure out the edges, and pray the city's still there." My ankle throbs, the sky hisses, but we start walking anyway. We trudge through a world scraped raw.

Derrick keeps his eyes on the sky while I sweep the wasteland for anything that may feed us. There is nothing but wind-born grit and the green flicker of rift lightning. The smog hangs so thick it feels alive, hiding any ship until its keel is scraping the dunes. Hours pass. Time has no meaning here, and the sun is a smear behind poisoned clouds, neither rising nor setting, only dimming by degrees.

When the ache in my throat turns to fire, Derrick pulls out the last canvas flask. We trade it back and forth, pretending each swallow is equal. I catch him palming the mouthpiece, letting the water wet his lips but not his tongue. I love and hate him for that. It makes me want to pour the whole flask into the dust just so we can be honest about how doomed we are. Then he tugs at my sleeve and points.

A leviathan of an airship sinks through the smog. We break into a run, hearts pounding with something that might be hope. Up close, the hull looms like the ribcage of a dead god. No deckhands shout warnings, no engines cough.

"Hello!" Derrick calls. The word dies against the steel. A rope ladder uncoils and an old man descends. His skin is stretched thin and eyes are hollow.

"Sir, are you all right?" My voice feels too loud. He studies us, lips cracked into something that might once have been a smile. "I'm Skye Talbot of The Raven, and this is Derrick," I gesture. "We can help with navigation, repairs, or anything."

A dry laugh rattles out of him. "Figures it'd be The Raven..." He turns, staring toward the endless wastes. Lightning ghosts across the horizon.

"We're heading for the city," I say, though I'm no longer sure it exists. "You could come with us."

"There's nothing left anywhere," he murmurs.

Derrick steps forward. "Do you have supplies? Even a little water?"

The old man's eyes flare, a last ember of temper. "I don't repeat myself, boy." Then he walks past us, feet whispering through the dust, moving toward the place where the land ends and the void begins.

"That way is only death," Derrick calls after him.

"Death comes for us all," comes the reply.

I raise my voice once more. "At least give us a name to remember."

"Captain Barnabas Hawthorn," he says, almost to himself. "Of the Skyward☐Seraph." He keeps walking until the gloom folds around him and even the lightning can't find his outline and we are left with the silence.

We trudge on until our limbs no longer work. The land coughs up the ghost of a city with charred walls and window frames like eye sockets. If this is the outskirts of the city, then Barnabas was right: there's nothing left.

"We have to stop," Derrick murmurs.

He's right. Push another step and we'll shatter. We check for injuries, then Derrick shakes out his spare shirt and spreads it on the rubble for a semblance of a bed. We lie shoulder to shoulder, staring at a sky that hasn't shown stars in years. I pretend the Atlantic murmurs somewhere behind the horizon, that salt is what stings my lips, not alkali dust. Derrick shifts, rolling toward me, and I turn to meet him. The world narrows to the breath between our mouths.

His eyes are hollowed by fatigue, bright with something reckless. This place and time can't cradle love. We both know it, the knowledge thrums like a warning wire, but want flares anyway, sharp and aching. He slips an arm around my waist and pulls me into the warm circle of his body. I let myself fit there, just for the length of one sigh. Tomorrow we'll rise (or we won't), but for tonight I borrow the luxury of his heartbeat against mine.

Derrick's breathing settles into the slow rhythm of exhausted sleep, but rest won't come for me. I ease off the scrap of shirt, step beyond the circle of his warmth, and tug the tome from the inside pocket of my coat. The glyphs whirl like migrating stars, demanding I tilt my thoughts, not just the page, to catch their drift. They speak of thread-singers that are beings who carry the first vibration of their birthplace in their marrow. When that note rings true, the skin between worlds thins, and the traveler slips through the hush between heartbeats. But if the note falters, lattices of possibility knot, seasons snarl into themselves, and the sky births ragged mouths that swallow whatever lingers near. One warning is carved so deep it punctures the vellum beneath:

To open a door is to owe the world a hinge.

Leave it unhinged, and you must become the nail.

I read it again and again until the words taste like iron. Every crossing is a debt: close the wound or let my bones be the pin that keeps reality from unraveling. Snapping the tome shut, I tuck it away and listen. The metallic whine that's haunted me since dusk rises in the distance, impossible to ignore. I leave Derrick to his dreams and follow the sound into the night.

Beyond the ruins, the ground splits, a hair-thin fissure that glows in the moonlight. I crouch and lay my palm against it. The wind is just gone and silence is so absolute it feels like being locked out of the world. Even the ash hangs motionless. The crack is cold at first, then greedy: strands of light seep from my skin, silver, then violet, then the sickly green of the stormed sky. It bleeds into the wound as though my body were a punctured vein. The rift drinks faster, widening, and something inside me stretches, eager to pour itself out.

A rush of vertigo swamps my senses. So this is the hinge, I think, pulse skittering. And I'm already half a nail. I don't want to die or disappear into some crack in the world, but if this is what it takes to hold it together, then I'll give what I can. The pull deepens; my fingers numb, elbow tingles. I try to break contact, but it does not let go.

"Skye!" Derrick's voice is raw with sleep. He's beside me, hauling at my shoulders. "What are you doing? Let go!"

"I can't," I gasp.

He braces a boot against the rock, pulls with all his weight, and my hand rips free. We sprawl on the dust, coughing. Behind us, the fissure shrinks to a dim pulse, as though it's licking its lips.

Derrick grips my wrists, searching my face. His hands are shaking. "You weren't yourself," he says, voice hoarse. "It was like you were breaking apart just to hold the world together. What in the Broken Hells was that?"

I flex tingling fingers, watching light fade beneath my skin. "The book says every door we open needs a hinge," I murmur, still shaking.

Derrick's confusion flickers into fear. "Then we keep you away from the doors."

I shake my head, eyes on the throbbing seam. "No. We need to learn how to close them before they decide I'm the easiest way to stay open."

"Maybe it was a bad idea to leave Micah and Muirenn behind." Derrick suggests. I turn away and he steps in front of me. "If you'd stayed one more second..."

"Then I'd be gone. Point taken. We're moving." I shoulder past him toward the dead horizon. "Save the lecture for someone who cares." Behind me, he swears under his breath, but his footsteps fall in line. The crack gives a final, greedy twitch, and I don't look back. It starts as a flicker, a shimmer on the horizon. This time it is not lightning, but something real. "Derrick," I choke out, my throat shredded. "There. Look!"

He lifts his head. His eyes catch the glow. "The city," he breathes. "It's still - "

"We don't know that." But we're already running. We run like the world's chasing us, because it is. The storm is behind us, moving fast. Our legs are shaking, lungs raw, feet blistered to ribbons, but that light pulls us like a lifeline. Maybe it's a flare or reflection on glass. I don't care. It's a chance. Hope is dangerous, but I want it anyway.

The closer we get, the slower it flickers. Steady and golden. But when we reach it, there's only ash and cinders. The blackened ribs of a fire, half-buried in collapsed stone. The sound that claws its way out of me doesn't feel human. I fall to my knees and scream until there's no air left and Derrick's arms lock around me, his body trembling against mine. He doesn't say anything.

Something happened, a rift quake, maybe. I can feel it under my palms and in my bones. The power is still here, lurking beneath the charred ground. It feels sinister and hungry, but not dead. Maybe I can use it.

"I don't think there's anything left to fight for," I whisper, my voice a scraped-out shell.

Derrick nods. His lips are cracked, blood on his teeth. "Can you get us out?"

"All I can do is try."

I press my palm to the scorched earth like before. The response is instant, like the world's claws dragging me under. Magic floods through me, and my spine locks. I can feel it ripping inside, churning blood and memories. Then I see it. Home. Not The Broken Lands, but my other home in Portsmouth. Wind and salt and gulls over the Atlantic. The air shimmers in front of me and splits as a sliver of space peels open, a gash of light and impossible blue.

"Derrick!" I yell. "Grab my hand!" He does and the rift roars. We take one step and the sky detonates. A bolt of green lightning rips from the clouds and slams into me, straight through my chest. My vision goes white. My body convulses, seizing with light and pain and screaming static. Derrick's hand jerks in mine and then he goes limp. His body crashes to the ground.

"No!" I drop beside him, shaking so hard I can hardly hold him. His eyes are closed. Blood trickles from one nostril. I scream his name until my throat splits, but he doesn't stir. Then I try to drag him to the rift, the one I made, but it's already closing. The light vanishes, and the silence that follows is final, sealing the sky.

When the storm moves in, it is ready. The ground quakes beneath us, and my power is gone. I am burned through like a fuse. I couldn't open another way even if I wanted to. This is how it ends. I cradle Derrick in my arms and press a kiss to his brow, then to his mouth, all while trying to memorize him before the void takes us both.

"Sorry," I whisper. "I was supposed to save you."

The storm begins to scream, but it is not the wind I hear, its engines. A shadow cuts through the haze, carving through the ash-choked sky like a blade. Lights blaze. Metal gleams. I know that shape, that sound -

The Raven.

She drops out of the clouds like a war cry. Scorched, battered, and beautiful. I sob. I scream. I wave my arms, body wracked and broken, mouth open in a cry that's more animal than girl. They came back. Not all hope is a lie.

CHAPTER 25

The strong arms of a crew member I don't recognize haul me onto the deck of The Raven. A moment later, they secure a rope to Derrick and begin lifting him up with practiced ease.

Lena sprints toward me, pulling me into a tight embrace. "I was so worried, little bird."

My mother stands at the far end of the deck, arms folded, eyes black as night. Her posture is rigid as she looks me over. For a heartbeat, her hand twitches at her side, almost reaches for me, but she shoves it into the folds of her coat instead and turns away. It is like she's evaluating a trade, not a daughter. I hate her for that, and I hate how I can't stop looking back.

"Come see me when you've cleaned this up," she says over her shoulder. I'm not sure if she's talking to Lena or to me.

"Take Derrick to the doctor," Lena instructs.

I blink. "Wait. Since when do we have a doctor?"

Lena's gaze clouds, and though she schools her expression into calm, I catch the flash of pain beneath it. "You've been gone a long time, child. We've gained many aboard The Raven since then." She looks like she wants to say more, but doesn't.

"My mother would never keep a doctor. She has you for that."

Lena sighs. "The Raven is one of the last airships left." The words hit like a blow. My chest goes tight.

"That can't be," I whisper. "The sky was full of them."

"It was," she says gently. "Six months ago."

"But - " I choke on the word, trying to gather my thoughts. Micah warned me time moves differently in the caverns, but could six months really change the world this much?

"We're running out of time," Lena says. A single tear tracks down her cheek. "We thought you and Derrick were dead. It was only Mira who insisted we keep searching. And we're blessed she did." I want to believe her. But I don't. My mother never cared. She was nothing if not practical. Lena sees the doubt written all over my face. "It's true," is all she says.

I change the subject. "Take me to Derrick."

Lena nods and leads me below deck, into the cramped living quarters of the crew. It's packed with people, and the stench is overwhelming: sweat, oil, and something sour lurking beneath it. The infirmary turns out to be just a repurposed cabin, one of the larger ones, but still tight and suffocating. A gaunt man looms over Derrick, his hands already in motion as he argues with a woman at his side.

"How am I supposed to treat him if I don't know what happened?"

"I told you, Dr. Venn," the woman snaps. "They just brought him in!"

"He was struck by rift lightning," I say, stepping in and pushing past them.

Dr. Venn turns to me, eyes narrowing. "Then he's already dead."

The room is too small for three people and all the ghosts hanging between us. I press my hands to Derrick's chest. His skin is clammy, but under my palms I feel that strange energy of something not quite alive, but not gone either.

I put a piece of myself into him. Just a thread and he stirs.

Dr. Venn takes a step back, eyes narrowing. "Witchcraft," he spits.

"Stuff it, Venn," Lena calls from the hall. Noted. They don't like each other.

Still, Dr. Venn casts one last look at Derrick and frowns. "He'll live. He just needs rest."

"There's nothing more you can do right now," Lena calls from the hall. "It's time to see your mother."

"And what if I say no?" As if that's ever been an option. My whole life was decided the day they brought me home. And now, after everything, I finally understand just how free my other life in Portsmouth really was. As lonely as I'd been, at least I was free. But I follow.

The table is set for three, just like the old days. I remember Derrick lingering like a shadow in his own home. My mother never let him sit with us. I'd accepted it then, but now I see it for what it was. Cruelty disguised as order.

"Just like old times," Mira says, forcing a smile. Something inside me cracks.

"I wanted to say thank you," I blurt out. "For rescuing us, and not giving up."

Mira doesn't look at me and sets her cup down with precision. "Don't."

"What?" I ask, unsure what just shifted.

"Act like gratitude makes up for it."

"I didn't - "

"You left, Skye." Her voice is calm. "And you didn't even say goodbye."

"You made it so easy to go.," I say, already feeling the heat rise.

Mira laughs. "Don't you dare put that on me. You–"

I flinch. "That's not fair - "

"Don't interrupt me." Her voice turns to ice. I bite my tongue and shrink into myself. "You disappeared and let us think you were dead. You don't get to waltz back in here with broken boots and tear tracks on your cheeks and expect me to pretend none of it happened."

"I'm not expecting that," I say, too fast. "I'm just trying to - "

"I said don't interrupt."

I sink back, and the silence between us thickens, bitter as old blood. I try to hold myself tall, to be strong, but it's slipping. All I wanted was for her to look at me and accept me, flaws and all. To say I was still hers and that I mattered. That I wasn't just a prophecy or some half-finished thing she regrets. Grace isn't something you can ask for. It has to be offered, and Mira has never given anything for free.

I remember once, when I was small, sitting outside her quarters with a broken toy in my lap. I didn't cry. I just waited, thinking if I was quiet and still and good, maybe she'd notice me. Maybe she'd care enough to ask why I was there. But the door never opened. The strength I've built since then doesn't help me here. Not against this. So I sit in silence, staring into the watery broth like it might anchor me. My throat burns. I swallow hard, but the ache doesn't go anywhere.

"Perhaps—" She starts, but we are interrupted by The Raven lurching.

Voices rise like a tide, louder with every word, and then the wind screams and is followed by a crack. The ship veers hard to port, and I slam into the wall. Somewhere, something shatters. Boots thunder across the deck above.

Mira grips my shoulder. "Stay here. Stay safe."

It's the way she says it that lights something furious in my chest. I'm not a child, and I am done being locked in place while the world tears itself apart. If I am the prophecy, then let me be, but before I can argue, she's gone. The ship's gears groan as I throw open the doors and climb to the deck. Rigging flails like wild vines, the sails whip in the wind. Crew scramble and shout, bodies braced against the chaos. Then a streak of rift-lightning rips across the sky and slams into the skeletal ruin of an old tower, not a quarter mile off the bow. The stones shimmer, then vanish in a blink of heat and shadow. What's left behind is... wrong. A hole in the air.

"Hold fast!" Mira's voice cuts through the wind. She's at the helm, hands on the wheel, jaw locked. "Lash it down!"

Lena stands just aft, arms wide, trying to speak to the wind, her voice swallowed by the storm. I run to a sail that slipped, and leap onto the rigging, fingers already raw, and grab the rope. The wind tries to rip me away, but I plant my feet and haul. Beside me, someone else grabs the line. We lock eyes just long enough to say everything and nothing. At some point, I find myself between my mother and Lena, a family fighting for survival.

A seam opens in the air just in front of me. It wavers, then sharpens. Inside it, we're there. Me. Mira, Lena, but not us. I've been here before, standing in front of the mirror in the cave, and my stomach lurches. Not again. They are twisted echoes of another time. Another version of us.

Their world bleeds through like ink in water. In it, the wind doesn't howl, it hisses, and the ground behind them is ash. Something burns in the distance, but the flames don't move as though the fire is frozen in time. They move in unison with limbs too fluid. I don't hear their voices, but I see their mouths shape silent words to one another.

Other Lena watches me with flat eyes while other Mira tips her head and smiles all wrong. The other Skye... winds help me, looks like something had hollowed her out and only hunger fills the space. They step forward together toward the seam.

My body knows before I do. If they come through, we'll merge just like before and maybe they want that, but the thing is... I don't. All I feel is dread. They look like salvation dressed in a skin of ruin. It's everything I could become if I chose wrong enough, long enough. I stagger back, bile rising in my throat. I reach out, hand trembling, and the seam pushes back, dragging at my fingers like it recognizes me, and wants me home. Part of me leans forward, yearning for something I can't name. A world where I don't have to fight so hard just to exist. Then I push harder until the surface snaps and the light devours my vision.

The wind vanishes all at once, and the air hangs still. The portal is gone. Above, the sails droop and all around me, the crew stands uncertain, waiting to be told what comes next. It takes a few heartbeats before movement stutters back into their limbs. Mira stands motionless for a moment, watching the place where the seam had been. Her face is unreadable. Then she turns on her heel and disappears below deck, boots striking hard against the wood. I don't follow.

Instead, I sink down where I stand, the grit of the deck biting into my palms as I press my hands against it like it might keep me from unraveling. I shake, hollowed out, but above me, the sky is clear. Lena sinks to the ground beside me, like she knows how close I am to shattering. Her arm slips around my shoulders. She doesn't say anything at first, just sits with me in the stillness the portal left behind. I don't know why that breaks me more than anything.

"She didn't even thank me," I whisper, my voice raw. "Why does she hate me?"

Lena exhales. "She doesn't hate you," she says. "She's just forgotten how to love." The words land, but I can't let them rest.

"I don't think she ever loved me," I say. "I was just a tool. A story she needed to shape into meaning."

Lena looks at me, and there's no judgment in her eyes. "She came for you because she loves you," she says. "But she's still learning how to say it." I want to believe her, but belief is slippery when you've spent your whole life being watched instead of seen.

My voice is a breath against the vastness overhead. "I don't want to beg for her acceptance." I pause. "But wind, I need it."

Lena's arm stays wrapped around me, grounding me. She doesn't offer false hope or tell me Mira will change, or that love is easy, or even possible. She just holds me. Maybe that's enough. I glance up at the sky and think of the faces behind the portal. The other me with the evil eyes, and I wonder how close I've come to becoming her.

Lena is still here. And for now... I'm still me.

CHAPTER 26

I go back to the room I grew up in and collapse onto the narrow bed, but sleep, if it comes at all, is fractured. Eventually, I give up and slip back to the deck. A skeleton crew keeps quiet watch as The Raven drifts south, her engines murmuring low, like she's tired too.

"Why aren't we going any faster?" I ask one of the men, a broad-shouldered deckhand with windburned skin and arms like tree trunks.

"We are," he says after a moment. "Storms chase us when we push too fast. This way... they fall behind." He's quiet after that. Then, almost as an afterthought, he adds, "Saw what you did last night. Always believed in you." No fanfare. Just a tip of his head before he returns to tightening lines. I freeze. It's such a passing kindness, but it sinks deeper than I expect. For so long, I'd thought I had to prove I mattered but maybe I already did.

I walk to the aft rail and look back at the nothingness we came from, the sky still rippling, and the world devoid of life. All at once, it hits me, the hopes and fears stitched into this ship, all orbiting the story of me. They had believed since I was a baby that I'd save them. Even when I told myself I was the child of prophecy, I don't think I ever believed it, not the way they do. I could barely close the rift last night, a seam in the air, nothing more, and that nearly destroyed me. How am I supposed to fix everything?

Behind me, the storm churns, unyielding, and I think I should have gone with Muirenn and Micah. They seemed so sure. They believed someone could help me understand what I am. I ran like I already knew the answers. Like a child pretending to be something more.

The version of me from the mirror world is seared into my mind. Her emptiness scares me more than I want to admit. How long before that becomes me? The decision comes quietly. It's already settled in my bones before I realize I've made it. I need to find the place the twins spoke of. Isdralan.

Derrick crosses my mind and I almost check in on him, but he'd just try to follow. He needs time to heal. If I somehow manage to save this world, there will be work to do. If I fail...

The pendant at my neck feels colder than I expect as my fingers close around it. I close my eyes. The Raven's frame hums under my feet, and I feel the metal thrum once against my skin, an old rhythm answering the new one rising in my chest.

Three crossings, maybe more, if you count the fractured pieces of me. Only one crossing was ever intentional. But if the book was right, if Isdralan runs in my blood like a memory, I can go there. I shove aside thoughts of the cave. Of Portsmouth. Of everything that tied me to any place I never truly belonged. Then, under my breath: Take me home. Half-expecting to need to click my heels three times, I open my eyes.

A seam has formed in the air, light bleeding through its edges like a sunrise caught in a crack. Beyond it: a forest, soft and humming with gold-filtered sunlight. The trees sway slow and strange, like they're breathing. The scent of moss and distant rain curls around me, familiar and impossible all at once.

Feet rooted to the deck, I hesitate. What if it's the wrong place? What if everyone there is like her - the mirror-me with nothing behind her eyes? What if I never make it back, or even want to? This world didn't do much for me and I've never belonged anywhere.

I step forward. Movement flickers to my left, and then a hand closes around my wrist. Before I can speak, the seam opens wide, and the world drops out from under me. Light swallows everything. Wind roars past, then vanishes. I'm falling - floating - becoming. The warmth is soft, wrapping around my ribs like breath.

Moss greets me like an old friend when I hit the ground. A second thump lands close beside me. Lying there, the light still pulsing in my veins, I stare up at a sky I've never seen, yet somehow, I know I'm where I was meant to be.

I roll onto my side to see what landed beside me. "Derrick!" He flashes a lopsided grin. "You could've been hurt! What if - " A fingertip presses to my lips, silencing my words before they spiral.

"I made you a promise," he says. "That I'd always be by your side."

"You were five," I snap, but it comes out too soft to sting.

He shouldn't have followed me again, but something in me settles. His presence calms me. I want to be angry, but I'm not.

I'm just… glad he's here, and that scares me. I need him, but part of me wonders how much longer he'll be able to follow where I'm going.

His hands frame my face, thumbs brushing my cheeks, and then his lips touch mine. I press closer, and the warmth gets in. Past the walls. Past everything, I thought I'd closed off. For a moment, there's nothing but this. Then I pull away. No. I have a duty, and there's no time for this. Not yet. Maybe when the world is saved. Regardless, I feel a spark of something inside me. Hope. Like there might be something after this and I don't have to be alone on the other side.

Derrick doesn't question. He just holds me for a while longer, until I slip from his arms and take in the surrounding land. This place is beautiful and wrong. It feels alive in a way that defies everything I've ever known. There's an energy in the air that hums beneath my skin, saturating everything. Magic, maybe, or something older. The trees seem to breathe, and the wind carries whispers. I wonder if this is what Lena hears when she listens.

Derrick steps beside me, eyes scanning the strange horizon. "This place feels like a strange dream," he murmurs.

In the distance, two figures emerge from the trees, their outlines softened by mist and golden light. My heart stirs. They're the right height, and familiar in the way their bodies move. It could be Micah and Muirenn, but as they draw closer, I'm filled with doubt. The man is older, marked by time. His dark hair is streaked with gray, and the lines around his eyes speak of years lived hard, and well. The woman beside him moves like wind over water, but there's something… distant about her.

They look like them, even feel like them. But they can't be. It's been less than a day. The man smiles. "Took you long enough."

I freeze. Micah, with that same dry humor in his eyes. Muirenn, quiet, like she's made of breath and memory. Both aged. I stare at him. "You're older," I say finally, because it's all I've got.

Micah chuckles. "Time's... different here. Doesn't really follow any rules.."

I step closer, voice cracking. "Can you help me? Please. I don't know what I'm doing. Everything's falling apart."

Muirenn studies me, like she's not just reading my face, but the pieces of me I've tried to hide. After a long silence, she shakes her head. "No," she says.

I blink, trying to find words. "Why not?"

Muirenn's voice is quiet. "You're close to the answers." Her gaze shifts toward the trees. "There's a place. Older than this forest, and Isdralan as we know it. The Heartroot."

I just listen.

"It was old when the world was still dreaming," she continues. "Some say it remembers before. You can speak to it if it chooses to hear you."

"Have you ever...?" I trail off.

Muirenn's voice falters. "I'm not one of the ones it speaks to."

I glance at Micah. "She's tried," he says. "We both have. But it isn't for us."

"Where is it?" I ask.

Micah rubs the back of his neck, glancing into the trees. "You'll find it if it wants to be found."

Muirenn adds, "It doesn't give answers. It gives the truth. Sometimes those aren't the same." Behind me, Derrick shifts, and I know if I turn, he'll be at my side, but this part isn't for him. Muirenn steps forward, expression unreadable. "We've gone as far as we're meant to." She places her hand lightly on my shoulder. It's warm and feels... final.

Micah steps beside her. "I never liked goodbyes." It sounds like he's said too many.

"Then don't say one," I whisper.

His eyes linger on me a moment longer, then he turns. I open my mouth to thank them, but the words feel too small, so I just watch them go. They walk together into the trees. Not vanishing. Just... dissolving into the golden mist, the way all old stories do. I want to run after them, ask them to stay and guide me, but that's not how this ends.

Then I turn to Derrick. His eyes are bright. He already knows what I'm going to say. "I have to go alone." For a second, I think he might argue. But he doesn't. "Will you wait?" I ask.

"I always do." He takes my hand and presses something into my palm. A cord with a carved piece of wood and a feather I'd given him when we were kids. I didn't even know he still had it. "For luck," he says. I don't trust my voice, so I just nod. I close my hand around it, like it might tether me, then step away before I can change my mind. When I look ahead, I see it. I could swear it wasn't there a moment ago, but now it's undeniable.

A tree, if you can call it that, rises amid the forest, vast enough to shatter the sky. Its trunk is wide as a house, bark glossy like old obsidian, etched with veins of light that pulse. Branches spiral upward beyond sight, disappearing into a canopy so high it might as well be the stars. And its roots vanish into the earth, as if they've wrapped around the bones of the world.

How had I missed this?

I look back at Derrick, who nods with encouragement, but he does not see what I do. As I move, the world tilts and the forest leans in. Trees stretch taller than they should, their branches curling like fingers and leaves ripple without wind. There's no path. Moss is worn in a line, a stone nudged aside and a gap in the undergrowth that looks more like suggestion than design. When I hesitate, something shifts as though beckoning.

The scent of earth rises thick and sweet. Honeysuckle, maybe, or just a memory. My feet are bare, though I don't remember removing my boots. Then I see it, a clearing, or maybe more of a hollow. It is ringed with roots and dappled light. I step inside, and it feels like walking into music.

She's already there.

A woman sits at the base of the Heartroot, back resting against the bark like she's grown there. Her hair is pale like mine, and falls in long, loose waves down her back. She doesn't move, but I feel her watching me. Not in the way predators watch, more like the moment before a question is asked. Her face is half in shadow, but even from this distance and a memory stirs. Some bone-deep recognition. I was just a baby when I lost her, but still... I know.

My birth mother.

That should be impossible. Maybe it is, but nothing in this place follows rules, and her face has been waiting in the quiet places of my mind all along. She doesn't speak, just waits, and so does the tree. There's no rush, but I can feel the expectation.

Like the world is holding out its hands and letting me decide whether I'll take them. I think about all the times I ran. From Mira, Lena and Derrick. From who I was supposed to be. I've always been good at running. But I didn't come here to run.

As I pass under the arch of roots that frame the hollow, a low-hanging branch brushes my shoulder. The leaves are soft as breath. One grazes the back of my hand and it feels alive. When the wind stirs, I swear it says my name.

CHAPTER 27

The woman sits with her back resting against the great tree. Her pale hair streams over her shoulders, catching the dappled sunlight, and her stillness is uncanny. She meets my eye and I freeze. Every part of this place feels trapped in time...

There's so much I want to ask. Who is she, where has she been, and oh so many whys. The words don't come. I squeeze my eyes shut, like that might hold me together, but my chest is tight with everything I've never said. Before I can speak, I hear her voice inside my mind.

"Ah, child... listen now, and I'll tell you a tale..."

It seems strange, but I don't ask any questions, and take a seat beside her, under the tree.

"There was a time," she starts. "Long before the world split, the land had but one heart.

In those days, at the center of all things, there stood a tree. Tall as forever, wide as longing. The First Tree, some say. The Heartroot, others whispered. But it had no name of its own, for it was memory. Not like that which we keep in our minds, but the deep kind. The kind that lives in the bones of the earth.

Now, they say a traveler came to that tree once. Not for power or glory, but for love. The seeker had lost someone, you see. A loss so vast, it left them hollow. They weren't ready to let go. They believed the Heartroot remembered everything. Even time and death. So they came with a single question.

Can I go back?

But the Heartroot does not give answers lightly, child. Not that question, nor any.

So the seeker gave what they had. First, they gave their voice, so their plea could not sound like a demand. Then they gave their sight, so they would not judge what they came to find. Then their name, so no one could call them back. The tree was silent. So they gave more.

Days. Years. Whatever passed for time beneath those great branches. They gave it willingly. Still, the tree did not answer. At the end, the seeker gave the only thing left: themselves. All of it. They let go, not just of who they were, but of why they'd come.

Only then did the Heartroot speak. The seeker did not return to the past. The dead did not rise. The wound of loss did not vanish. But the wound in the world closed. And the seeker? They became part of the tree's memory.

"Now, when the wind moves just so, and the leaves shiver like they know something you don't, if you listen closely, you might hear the shape of that question."

"What was the answer?" I ask.

"That's still coming," she says. Her lips move, but I only hear the voice in my head. "So now you stand where the seeker once stood. The wind knows your name. The roots have heard your steps. The tree will not ask you what you want. It already knows. The only question now is, what will you give?"

I want to scream or throw something. Perhaps just march right up to the tree, slap it across the bark, and demand a different story. One where I get to be a person and not a symbol. One where I get to live - because I am so tired of being the story everyone else tells.

I press my hands into the moss, and it breathes beneath my fingers. Of course it does. Everything here is alive and waiting for me to become something more than I ever asked to be. It isn't fair. I never asked to be born into prophecy. I never agreed to save anyone, and I sure as hell didn't volunteer to be scattered across timelines and stitched back together.

"Why me?" I ask. "Who the hell am I supposed to be and why do I have to be the one to give up everything? Why not someone else?" The branches above shifted like they pitied me. Then, quieter, I ask. "Where did I come from?"

The woman smiles and I hear her voice in my head again. "I'll tell you another tale. There was once a girl, or perhaps she was a star that hadn't yet remembered how to burn. No one's sure what she was, only that she wasn't meant to stay. She was born in a place the wind can't reach and where breath and light were the same thing. Names were not worn but sung. They say she danced in the rivers between worlds, but even stars can be curious.

One day, she slipped through a crack in the world and landed somewhere dark. At first, she marveled at the strangeness. The taste of salt and the ache of breath. She discovered hands she hadn't had before, and eyes that could close. She found time, and oh, child, time is a thief. It wears like a river against stone. The girl forgot the light that used to wake inside her when she laughed.

She learned sorrow, and hunger, and stories that began with "once" instead of "always." She learned to survive. Still buried deep in her bones, something remained. There was a song, deep inside her like breath held too long, a tiny seed. Sometimes, when the wind shifted just right, or the sky broke open with storm, she would almost remember, but almost is not becoming."

The woman's voice dropped to a hush. "So you ask where you came from, child. Who you are. Let me tell you the truth of it." Her gaze didn't waver. She rose and stepped closer. "That name you've been chasing? It's not a key, it's a root. You are not the girl who fell. You're the one who grows." She tilts her head, as if listening to something I can't hear. "So ask your questions, if you must, but ask like the seed does."

I stared at her and the words that didn't feel like answers. Ask like the seed does? What did that even mean? To wait in the dark and split yourself open, not knowing what would grow? I didn't want to be patient. I didn't want to reach blindly toward something I couldn't see, but I felt it as though I was remembering how to lean toward the light.

What if the light didn't want me?

There had been so much darkness in my life, but none was worse than my mother. Mira's lack of love was the sharpest wound I carried, even more than being invisible on earth. The tree had said to ask like a seed, but how does a seed ask why a mother couldn't love her child? If she hated me so much, why didn't she leave me to die? Was I ever anything more than a tool to her? A means to an end dressed up as prophecy?

I tried to form the words, but they wouldn't come. Mother stuck in my throat like ash, so I let the anger speak instead. "Why did The Raven hate me?" I ask.

"That's a deep cut you're pressing on." The woman replies. "The kind that doesn't bleed red. I know these stories too, the ones that taste like iron and silence. The stories mothers are not meant to pass on but do, anyway. Come close. Let me tell you of the woman who built a tower so tall, she forgot the shape of her own heart." She is sitting again, and I place myself in a patch of moss next to her.

"There was a woman once, not a queen, though she wore crowns, and not a god, though many begged her like one. She had no name anymore, only titles, but before all that, she was someone's daughter and she was afraid. Afraid of hunger, of chaos, of being small in a world too large. She was scared that love would not be enough and no one would come for her.

So she did what the world taught her to do: She built armor. Not from steel. No, she built her armor from control. She controlled her words, her people, her grief. She turned fear into rules and longing into law. They said she was strong, but they were wrong. She wasn't strong, she was fortified.

Then came a child, a miracle born of sky-stuff and secrets. The woman looked at her and something cracked open, because the child wasn't made of stone and silence. She was made of truth and light. Truth is dangerous to those who've hidden too long inside their own walls. So the woman didn't hold her, she caged her. She called it safety and prophecy, but deep down, it was fear. The child reminded her of the self she'd buried long ago, the one who cried, asked for help, the one who was never enough.

"Oh, child… sometimes we hurt what we love most, because we see in them the things we could never save in ourselves."

I close my eyes and shiver. I'd never let myself see her as human, only as a blade, but she wasn't a weapon. She was the wound itself, dressed in steel and pretending it gave her strength. Lena saw the fracture beneath the edge. She tried to tell me. I didn't listen.

The woman went on, "So why did she hate you, child? Because she couldn't bear to love you. Not as you were. Love would have broken the dam, and behind it, flows grief and shame. But listen well: that was her truth, not yours. You are not her ruin. You are the question she could not answer."

Her gaze sharpened. "And the truth, child, the one she feared most, is this: power cannot protect you from your own reflection. You've seen her now. The girl underneath, still hiding. You do not have to become her."

In that moment, I realize all I truly want for my mother is peace. In fortifying herself, she forgot how to love without fear. "She didn't hate me. She hated what I made her feel." I speak the words out loud, hoping to manifest them in Mira's heart, and something inside me shifts. A breath later, I ask, "Why did I split in two?"

The woman waits before answering. She is never in a hurry, but neither is the truth. "There was a creature once, neither god nor mortal, but something whole. It lived at the center of all things, not needing direction. Joy and sorrow moved through it like twin birds sharing a nest. It simply was. But the world began to pull at it with an aching hunger for healing, and this, the creature knew, required witness. So it did the only thing it could. It split.

Not from rage or fear, but to see more clearly. It fractured into two ways of seeing. One would walk through the wounds of the world. The other would remember the stars. They weren't halves, they were mirrors, each holding a piece the other could never carry alone. One bore the burden. The other kept the memory. They dreamed of each other because they were never meant to stay apart, only to be divided long enough to understand what division meant."

"What happens when they find each other again?" I ask, desperate to understand why.

"That," she answers, "is the harder tale. To reunite is not to rewind. It's not patching the crack or pretending the break never came. It is to transform. The self you were, the one you became, neither survives the joining untouched. They must die, child, to become whole."

I flinch and think of my other selves. Do they still exist somewhere out there, separate from me? This seems to be what Micah implied. *No.* They're gone, and I'll never get them back. Maybe that isn't a tragedy. Perhaps just a beginning. The shape of an answer is starting to form, a reason for why I'm here, but I'm afraid to look it in the eye.

Somewhere inside me is the version who just wanted to be enough. The girl who sat at the back of a classroom on Earth, invisible unless she was bleeding. Who dreamed, once, of being seen. She didn't get much, and now here I am, expected to hold whole worlds together when I could barely hold myself. I was a child, a prophecy, a liar, a ghost. I survived by fracturing into the pieces others needed. And somehow, every broken version of me led to this.

"How do I save my world?" I ask, already afraid I know the answer.

"You already have the answer," she replied. "I'll tell you a thing few have ever asked to hear, and fewer still have dared to understand. A story of becoming. There was a soul once, just a spark adrift. It longed, as all things do. So it took shape in fragments until it carried a name, a face, and a story.

It moved through the world, feeling joy and loss, craving things no food or drink could fill. It loved, and in doing so, it learned fear. It built walls, crafted quiet places to hide its hurt. Over time, it forgot what it had been. Its name became everything and scars felt like truth. Grief was the proof it had lived.

The world does not allow stillness for long. It shifted, and the soul cracked. It began to see things as they were. The river did not hold the fish, and the flame did not grieve the wood. The wind let the leaves fall. Nothing clung. Everything became. And so the soul wept. It remembered it was never meant to stand alone. It was meant to belong. To sky, to root, to wind, to wound, to wonder. Not as a god or a ghost, but as breath returned to the greater exhale of all things.

To let go of the self is the final and hardest gift. No one speaks your name. Your hands no longer shape the world. You leave behind not only the pain, but the story that held it. Still, it is not loss, it is return. Not upward, but inward, down into the heart of everything, where sorrow settles into stillness, where longing becomes light, where 'I' becomes 'We'."

I feel the shape of my story. Could I give it up? My pain, my shape, my name? I think about Derrick and the steadiness in his touch when everything else trembled. I could turn back. I could go to him. We could find some quiet place and pretend the rest of the world doesn't exist. I could lay this all down, just for a little while.

But, the truth is that even if I don't want to give everything, I already know I will. Not because some ancient tree is humming expectantly at me, but because someone has to give it. There's still a girl inside me who wants the world to be better, and for others to experience the world, even if I don't get to live in it.

I wrap my fingers around the feathered token Derrick gave me. It's small. Ridiculous, even. It doesn't have power, but it's real, and it's mine. I turn to the woman I thought was my mother, fists clenched at my sides. She's already fading into the bark behind her. Her shape becomes a memory.

There's something here I can't name. A sense that nothing was forgotten, and nothing needs to be. It settles deep into me and soothes the edges of my anger without erasing it. I am changed, but I'm still me. I touch the tree, and the knowing unfurls inside me. I have my answer. I turn and run, my footsteps swallowed by the moss, and the clearing fading behind me like a dream that gave more than it took.

Derrick stands where I left him, arms crossed, posture taut, like he's been trying not to pace. The moment he sees me, his shoulders drop in relief. I slow as I reach him. He doesn't say anything, just looks at me with that quiet intensity of his. I open my hand and show him the feather. Just a small thing, fragile and light, but it matters.

"I know what we need to do," I say. No explanation. He doesn't ask for one. He simply reaches out and takes my hand.

CHAPTER 28

The Raven was docked in the same place when we arrived, and I almost wonder if it had never left at all. The reality is my mother would not have stayed the whole time. She abhorred looking weak. I could see the rifts in the distance, and the city was overflowing with refugees. To the south was the wastelands. Nothing could live out there, and trying was a long, slow death sentence. I wonder if it had once been a vast ocean, like back home. For a moment I can see the great black gull circling overhead, untethered, then the land fades back to the wasteland it is.

My heart aches for this world. This desolate place that raised me, and the place my people broke. I think of Rhu and Vi and all those I left behind on my beautiful earth, and hope their world never gets to this point. Part of me is still afraid of what's coming. I inhale, smelling the memory of a sea breeze. Derrick is watching me. He doesn't know yet, but he suspects. It's him I will miss the most. Or will I? What is to come is unfathomable. Shaking off the moment, I approach the ship.

One of the crew points a weapon at me that looks a bit like a shotgun, and I wonder if the ship supplied it. I laugh to myself, knowing I would never have even known what a shotgun was, if it were not for my time on Earth. Then his eyes widen as he recognizes my pale hair.

"She is back," he cries, turning and running below deck. Derrick reaches out and squeezes my hand. I am not sure how this meeting with my mother will go. All I want is for her to feel the love she deserves.

She rushes to the deck and down the gangplank and sweeps me into her arms. Lena is right behind her. The three of us embrace into a hug and my heart breaks a little. I wonder where my mom and dad are, and if they mourn me? When I became whole again, did I cease to exist in that world? Part of me thinks it would make sense- I was always invisible there, but the love in my dad's eyes on the day I left spoke volumes. I would like to think that there is a piece of me in their hearts, even if they don't remember what it is.

"You came back." My mother's voice is thick with something I almost don't recognize, and for the first time, I see her without the black kohl lining her eyes. She looks... different. Softer. Or maybe just tired. The shift in her expression is subtle, but I see the way her face crumples. "You should have stayed safe."

Lena doesn't say anything at first, just tracks the horizon, her sharp gaze locking onto the rifts to the north. The sky is splitting open, unraveling itself. The world is out of time. When she looks at me, her expression is unreadable. "It won't be long now," she says. "The storms are coming."

"We searched for you," Mother whispers. "We scoured the lands." She says it like an accusation… or a prayer. Where did you go? It's only then that she sees Derrick. He's been standing just behind me, silent as a ghost. Her body tenses, but instead of the cold calculation I expect, she only dips her head. "Thank you," she murmurs. "For keeping her safe and bringing her home."

Then she does something I never would have predicted. She pulls him into a hug. Derrick stiffens at first, but she doesn't let go, and when she releases him, she says, "You deserved better." She turns to me. "You did too."

For a second, I don't know how to breathe. I want to ask her why now? What happened in my absence that softened her edges? But I don't have to look far for the answer.

The sky has split apart. The end is coming. Everyone left has migrated to the city, clinging to the last scrap of shelter before the storms claim what's left of the world. There is nowhere else to go.

I press a kiss to Derrick's forehead. It's a quiet, final thing. "I need a moment with Mira and Lena."

Derrick hesitates, my choice of words not lost on him. I see it in the flicker of recognition, in the way his eyebrows twitch upward, almost amused. It reminds me of when we were kids, of a time before any of this mattered. He exhales, then inclines his head, slipping away toward his old room, leaving me with the women who raised me.

I face them, the weight of everything settling over me. How does one say goodbye without saying goodbye? I am not sure they would understand what I need to do, and I can't risk them stopping me. But this me, the version of myself that still belongs to them, she needs closure. Our story started when they rescued me. When I became their child of prophecy. Now, it has to end.

"I wish you had stayed where you were safe." Mother reaches out, fingertips grazing my cheek.

Lena doesn't say anything. Just watches. Like she knows. Wind blows at my hair and I brush it out of my eyes. The world is unraveling piece by piece, and yet, with them, it feels like nothing has changed. Like I'm still that baby they found. Lena leans against the wall, watching me with that quiet, knowing gaze.

Mira paces, her hands twitching like they want to grab something. Control, certainty maybe, and a solution. She settles for words instead. "You should have stayed where you were safe," she says, voice edged with frustration. "Wherever you were, I bet they–" She cuts herself off.

I arch a brow. "Loved me?" I challenge. "Cared about me?"

Mira scoffs. "I was going to say I needed you."

Lena's fingers drum against her arm as she studies me. She doesn't speak right away, which is worse than anything Mira could say. "Lena," I say, because I need her to fill the silence.

Her lips press into a thin line. "You look different."

I swallow. "It's been a long month." She doesn't buy it.

"This sounds like a goodbye," Mira exhales. "You just got back, and now you're acting like you've got one foot out the door." My heart stutters. Mira has no idea how right she is.

"I just know what's coming," I say, voice softer than I mean for it to be. "Perhaps I wanted to see you both before - " I stop myself.

Mira's eyes flash. "Don't do that."

"Do what?"

"Talk like it's over," she snaps. "Like you already know how this ends."

Her words hit too close, so I deflect. "You never liked prophecies, did you?"

"Prophecies are for people waiting to be saved," she bites back. "We save ourselves."

I should let it go. I don't. "And if saving ourselves means making up prophecies?"

Mira stills. Lena shifts beside me and doesn't speak for a long time. Then she says, "Tell me, Skye, if you had to choose, would you rather survive or be free?" I blink at her. The question is a trap.

Mira scoffs. "Survival is freedom, Lena." Lena doesn't look at her. She looks at me.

I think of what's coming. Of the storms, the rift swallows the world whole. Of the way the winds whisper, how they already know what I've chosen. I think of them. The people I love. Then I lie. "I guess I'll have to find out."

Lena exhales through her nose, the closest she'll ever come to calling me a liar to my face.

Mira rubs a hand over her jaw, then shakes her head. "Enough talking in riddles. We move at first light." There it is. The assumption is that I'll be here in the morning. I press my hands to my sides, steadying myself. I glance at them and force a smile.

"Good night," I say, voice steady. "I love you." Mira flinches like she wants to say it back but doesn't know how. Lena leans in and brushes her hand lightly against my sleeve.

"You were never alone," Lena says softly. "We have loved you even when we didn't know how to show it."

For a heartbeat, I think Mira might echo it. Her hand lifts slightly, then falls, but her eyes shine with unshed tears. "Go to sleep," she mutters.

"We'll see you in the morning." Lena adds.

The lie sits between us, but neither of them knows it's a lie. Then they turn and go, their footsteps fading into the night. I let out a slow breath. Then I turn toward my own room and walk into the last goodbye I hadn't planned for.

Derrick is sitting on my bed. "You have something planned, don't you?" he asks.

I don't flinch. Just tilt my head, keep my voice easy. "I'm working on it." Another lie. I've told more lies today than in all my lives combined.

He narrows his eyes but lets it go. "Will you tell me when you figure it out?"

"Of Course."

I see it in his face: he knows I'm lying. He lets me do it anyway, because loving me has always meant carrying the weight of the things I won't say. Then, I close the space between us and press my lips to his. His breath hitches, eyes widening in surprise. The last time we were in this situation, I was trying to manipulate him, and he was too scared of my mother to know what to do with me. The memory makes me want to laugh and cry at the same time.

But this? This isn't like before. This time, he melts into me.

It's not a passionate kiss, but something deeper. I pour myself into it. Everything I am, everything I will never be. The ache of being unseen, the hollow ache of being the one who will save us all. It is ironic that, in the end, it will be me. I fill the kiss with things I learned in Isdralan, the weight of knowing, the loneliness that's always been waiting for me.

I give it all to him.

Then we collapse into the bed, arms and legs tangled together, holding each other like we're the last solid thing in a world slipping away. I stare at him for a long time, memorizing his shape, and the quiet way his chest rises and falls. Our eyes shut, and for a moment, I think about staying until morning. But I know if I do, I'll never be brave enough

Instead, I press one last kiss to his forehead, slip out of his hold, and grab my wings. I know I don't need them, but they feel like the only thing that's ever been mine. On the deck, the night stretches open around me. A gust of wind hums low and steady, like a voice older than time. I walk to the figurehead and press my hand against its beak. The ship wakes at my touch. It has always known me.

Then The Raven rises, silent as breath, and slips from the dock without a whisper. Below, the crew sleeps. Whether it's magic that holds them in their dreams or simply the absence of the engines' familiar roar, I don't know. I only know that no one wakes.

Higher and higher, it climbs into the night, slicing through the clouds. The stars stretch out before me, gleaming like scattered embers, and my pulse slows. We veer north toward the largest of the rifts. I tighten the straps of my wings and inhale. Then I step into the void.

I understand now. This isn't because I was born for it, or because some prophecy demands it. It's because I chose it. I have seen enough sorrow to know the world deserves more than endings. It deserves becoming. I knew before, but not like this. Not with the certainty that radiates beneath my skin and pulls me like the tide. The sky bends around me, stretching, folding, making space where there was none before.

My fingers unravel first, the hands that reached, that held, that fought and failed and tried. Then my feet, the ones that ran across two lives, two selves, a story that was never supposed to be divided. The space between my ribs stretches wide, no longer a hollow ache, but something vast and full. I feel the breath of the wind, the pulse of the storm, the weight of the ocean pressing against the shore. The world is inside me. Or maybe I am inside it.

My memory is the last thing to go. I think of Mira's fire, Lena's patience, Derrick's quiet, steady presence, and try to hold on to them. They slip away, not because they are gone, but because I am too much to hold.

I do not close the rift, I become, and feel myself stitching the great tears. The storm exhales. The sky settles.

And I...We... are not Skye.

We are not names or bodies or self. We are the current and the still, the silence and the roar, and the breath between what was and what will be.

We are everything.

And we are nothing at all.

CHAPTER 29

The Raven rarely left the sky docks these days. Not because it couldn't fly, Derrick was as good a captain as any, but because the world no longer needed to be saved. Life was... different. Calmer, yes, but also emptier. Part of him wished things had ended another way. Very few knew the price their child of prophecy had paid: just himself, Mira, and Lena. Probably Micah and Muirenn too, wherever they were. He wasn't even sure Skye thought of it as a sacrifice.

Derrick leaned against The Raven's railing, staring out over the mended skyline. The rifts were gone now, and the sky below was as blue as the one above. Even from here, he could see people rebuilding city walls, planting new farms, forging new alliances. There was even an honest-to-goodness ocean to the south. The land was healing.

He closed his eyes for a moment, letting the breeze lift his hair. Sometimes he imagined it was her fingers brushing past. Maybe it was. It didn't matter. She was part of this world now, stitched into its breath and bone. He rested a hand on the polished planks beneath his feet and exhaled, the familiar wood steady beneath his palm.

One year, and he could still see her stepping off into the night. Should he have followed her or tried to stop her? Maybe part of loving someone meant trusting their final leap.

"Captain?" The bosun interrupted his thoughts.

"Yes?"

"Crew's loaded the last crates. Where do you want 'em?"

Derrick blinked, dragging himself back to the present. "Oh... Lash them in the hold. We'll keep 'em there until we head north next week."

The man grunted and handed him the packing slips. Derrick tucked them into his pocket and smiled at the normalcy. Next week's run would be a routine one: medical supplies and fresh produce to a small settlement getting back on its feet. If only Skye could see him now, sorting seeds and cloth instead of outrunning storms (or pining after her.)

Mira and Lena had retired from air travel, though they dropped by sometimes with updates from the city. It had been renamed Ravenshearth, to honor The Raven's role in the world's healing. Mira still couldn't resist fiddling with the ship's gears, barking out orders before remembering she wasn't in charge anymore. Lena would only watch her with that familiar half-smile, the kind you gave to people you loved even when they made you crazy. Somehow, they had found their peace together. It was messy, prickly, and imperfect, but it was real.

Derrick still felt like he was waiting for something. Perhaps he always would. Part of hope was waiting, even when you didn't know what for. He scanned the cargo manifest to keep busy.

That's when he noticed someone standing at the far edge of the docks.

The woman was slight in build but carried herself like she owned the place. She wore scuffed boots and an old, rather odd coat. She took her time strolling along The Raven's length, reaching out every so often to touch it, like she was greeting an old friend.

Derrick squinted. "Can I help you?" he called.

The woman turned, an auburn ponytail swishing against her back. A silver hoop glinted at her ear. She held herself with a casual confidence, yet there was a restlessness about her too, like a coiled spring ready to snap.

"I heard The Raven might be needin' crew," she said without preamble. "I'm handy with knots, rigging... general deck work." Knots weren't the usual currency on an airship, but she didn't look out of her depth.

"What's your name?" he asked.

"Aanee."

There was a quiet steel in her tone, a self-assurance that made you want to lean in, waiting for her next words. Derrick felt a smile tug at one corner of his mouth. He'd met plenty of runaways, but Aanee didn't seem to be running. More like she was looking for something.

"All right, Aanee. We're mostly hauling supplies these days, not chasing the sky."

She nodded, giving The Raven's deck an almost affectionate glance. "That suits me."

He raised an eyebrow. "Are you running from trouble?"

Aanee gave a sly smile. "Not exactly. I just... don't mind a quiet routine now and again."

A breeze drifted by then, carrying the scent of salt and something wilder. It lifted Derrick's hair, and for a heartbeat he could almost hear Skye's laugh riding the wind. Or maybe it was just the ship, remembering her too.

"We pay a fair wage," Derrick said. "It's not glamorous."

"Glamour's overrated," Aanee said. "Besides, I like a good deck under my feet."

He chuckled, feeling something warm uncurl in his chest for the first time in a long while. "All right, let me show you around. Climb aboard."

Engines purred as Aanee set foot on deck. The Raven seemed to sigh, almost like she approved. Derrick guided her through a quick orientation: where supplies were stowed, the basics of safety, how the sails worked if the engine ever failed. She listened, nodding at each point, quick to learn and focused as she took in the ship's workings. When they reached the bow, Aanee ran her hand over the figurehead and whispered something inaudible.

"What was that?" Derrick asked.

"Just admiring the craftsmanship," she said casually. "I like to get a feel for a ship."

The breeze stirred again and Derrick chose to believe it meant something. They stood in a companionable hush as sunrise turned the sky gold. At last, he turned to her. "We can always use steady hands. If you're sure you want the job, it's yours."

Aanee tilted her head in acknowledgment. "I'm sure."

When he held out his hand, she clasped it firmly. An odd warmth tingled through his palm. "Welcome aboard," he said.

Derrick turned back to the horizon, letting Skye's memory settle inside him.

He had responsibilities now: a new crewmate to train, another journey to begin. One day at a time. Healing wasn't forgetting. It was flying anyway. Before him, the open sky. Behind him, the ghost of a girl stepping into the wind. This time, he didn't chase. He simply sailed.

"All right, Raven," he murmured. "Let's see where the wind takes us next."

In the distance, a seagull cried, its wings carving silver against the brightening sky. The world was still imperfect and full of storms, but for the first time in a long while, Derrick thought maybe it was enough.

Another story was beginning, because endings were never meant to last forever.

About the Author

Beth Connor is the author of Nexus of Sky, the Isdralan Chronicles, and the Kindred Spirits Mysteries.

Her stories blend speculative fiction with myth, memory, and emotional depth—exploring themes of identity, resistance, and the power of found family. She is also the creator of Crossroads Cantina, a genre-spanning fiction podcast, and a contributor to numerous anthologies and audio projects.

ALSO BY

ALSO BY BETH CONNOR:

Hollow City
Lake 40

<u>The Isdralan Chronicles:</u>
Micah and the Candles of Time
Prodigy of Flame
Bridge of Blood and Thornes

<u>Kindred Spirit Mysteries:</u>
The Secret of Misthaven Island
Bridging the Heart
The Curse at White Pines
The Last Act
I'll Be Home For Christmas